THE RAT PAPERS

Leaked and Almost Completely Redacted

CHRISTOPHER E. METZGER

authorHOUSE

AuthorHouse™
1663 Liberty Drive
Bloomington, IN 47403
www.authorhouse.com
Phone: 833-262-8899

Published by AuthorHouse 10/29/2020

ISBN: 978-1-6655-0564-2 (sc)
ISBN: 978-1-6655-0562-8 (hc)
ISBN: 978-1-6655-0563-5 (e)

Library of Congress Control Number: 2020921059

Print information available on the last page.

Any people depicted in stock imagery provided by Getty Images are models, and such images are being used for illustrative purposes only. Certain stock imagery © Getty Images.

Interior Graphics/Art Credit: Greg Gilmore

This book is printed on acid-free paper.

For Pam Jarrett

ACKNOWLEDGMENTS

- I thank Greg Gilmore for his drawings of my rats.
- I thank The Writers Group of Herndon, VA. for listening to the pre-published reading of THE RAT PAPERS.
- I thank my wife, Pam Jarrett, for her editing, her pushing me to publish this book, and her occasional attempts at giving me space while I wrote.
- I thank Benedict and Mathuzala for their help, without which this story may never have been told.

PREFACE

Call me Benedict.

I saved the life of a bug today. Yes, I did. Instead of killing it dead on the bathroom floor, I cupped it in my hand and threw it out my living room window; where it can try to reconnoiter with its kind, or chew on a leaf, or do whatever it wants to do out there. Whether or not it hooks up with its family or friends is really not my concern. All I know is, I gave it a second chance at life. Why do I tell you this? So, you can appreciate what a nice guy I am.

Some of the poorly informed will call me a traitor, or worse. Of course, there will be those who will accuse me of murder, but when you read my story, I am confident you will find me innocent by way of self-defense, or maybe by temporary insanity. At worst, I am guilty of 'Unintentional Manslaughter', if there is such a thing.

I do not know what kind of bug it was. Probably one of those new bugs that came over here on a container ship from China. No matter how they got here, they are ruining a lot of our crops. Soybeans and all sorts of fruit trees are in peril because of them. It goes to show you the problems that can come from this Globalization business. Maybe I should have squished the thing. It can get confusing.

But I am not here to talk about bugs, at least not at this telling. I am here to talk about Rats.

CHAPTER 1

RATS

"We cannot afford your 'Civilization' anymore, can we?" – Mathuzala, *(Who you will meet in later Chapters)* from his column in: https://notesfromtheroomofwonder.com

It was not the best of times; but hardly anyone knew it. People are like that. They have a tendency to think they are doing alright, when in fact they are quite miserable. Somebody had to do something - and that somebody turned out to be me.

Yes, I know the quality of life seems to have deteriorated since I got involved - but if it were not for me, well, the situation down on the ground would be even more insufferable.

Years ago, as a young man, way back in Junior High School, I had become intrigued by the experiments we, and when I say 'we', I mean we *humans*, were doing on animals for the benefit of scientific advancement. In particular, I was fascinated by the ones done on rats. No; more than fascinated make that: I had become *obsessed* by them. It was my calling. To have a calling can be a blessing. Or not.

One of the first experiments I read about was where the scientists took a group of rats and made them fat by stuffing them full of carbs and sugary sweet things. They took another batch of rats and fed them a proper diet, a diet from the good food group pyramid – which brought the members of this second pack to a lean and fit state of health. Then they dieted the fat rats to equal the weight of the thin. Next, they fed all of the rats the same healthy diet - and guess what? The rats who had once been fat, got fat again and the others remained thin. "*HHHmmm*," I remember thinking.

The second experiment I read about concerned Random Negative Re-Enforcement, in which a rat is placed in a maze and a piece of cheese is dangled at the end of the course. The rat finds the cheese. He is timed. Then the cheese is moved. He finds it. Timed again. Then they put electric shocks in the walls of the maze. Each time the rat takes the wrong pathway, he gets an electric shock. The walls tell him when he is wrong; and he learns. The clever rat finds the cheese, and each time he hits the course, (The "*trackus Rodentia*", as the witty lab-techs called it.) ...each time, there are fewer and fewer shocks to his tiny nose, or ribcage. Then they put the shocks in the walls in a way which do not relate to the pathway to the cheese, or to anywhere in particular - the shocking walls are placed at random. Eventually, the rat goes insane. The lab-techs then time how long it takes the rat to go insane. "*HHHmmm*," I thought.

Or, how about the infamous study where they put a rat in a cage and made it so that every time he struck a designated lever he got food? Soon, the rat learned to strike the lever when he was hungry. Then the lab-tech gave the rat cocaine when he struck lever numbered "Two". In quick time, the rat always went for the cocaine. Then they took away the cocaine, but the rat kept striking the lever numbered "Two", hoping to get his fix. He died of starvation, even though he could have struck for food an inch away. The record was: One rat hit the cocaine lever 122,462 times before he finally died. "*HHHmmm*," I kept thinking.

Mind you, I was only in Junior High when I was exposed to these ingenious studies. Young and impressionable, I could not get enough of them. Over time, I became a proficient, scrounging 'techie' - capable of searching the internet and, eventually, its cloud and capturing any data, anywhere in the world which related to the subject of Man/Rat Studies.

Fast forward through College... a master's in computer science... Working on Wall Street in the arena of Cyber-security...

I was living in Manhattan during one of their Great Garbage Strikes. Bags of garbage were stacked head-high on the sidewalks. At night, rats were above ground and all over the City. It is said there was one rat per person in the Borough before this particular strike - and two rats per capita when the strike was over. The garbage pick-up/shut down was a food feasting, romantic interlude for the rats. One night, while walking home from Allen's Pub up on 73rd and 3rd, I noticed several rats staring at me. Just a couple of them, stopped in their tracks, gazing at me as I went by. The next night there were a few more...and the whole pack followed me for several yards. On the third night, about fifty of them tracked me all the way to my doorstep. "*HHHmmm,*" I thought.

For several months I sat on the back stoop of my brownstone looking at the rats, which, or who, had followed me home each night - and they sat and stared back at me. (I had taken to holding these sessions at the darkened backside of my apartment building; to avoid intrusive onlookers.) At first, I had mixed feelings about these meetings, for the thought had occurred to me the rats were looking at me because I am a peculiar looking person. My face sort of protrudes to an elongated point because of a traumatic birth experience. If you were to look at my profile, you might notice the whole shape of my face seems to follow the end point of my nose. My mother, who was not a good mother by any stretch of the imagination, never spent so much as a penny on fixing my horribly bucked teeth. Since childhood, I had been ostracized by my peers, due to my facial appearance. I have adjusted to this distinction and have come to realize I am actually better off than many of those who are quite 'normal'. However, due to my physical presentation you can understand why I wondered about the motives of the rats' curiosity towards me.

It turns out my new friends were trying to communicate with me.

They can talk, you know. Yes. Not like we do, with our tongue and whatever; but they twitch their noses and move their mouths and whiskers methodically and they make little screeching sounds from the back of their throats. I mimicked them and found I, too, could twitch my nose and upper lip and make little screeching sounds from the back of my throat. After an amazingly short period of time I grasped the basic elements of their language. It was not long before I was fluent. I guess I am a natural born linguist. Lucky me.

Here are some of the things we talked about in our earlier conversations:

One, they told me they were not responsible for the Plague. The bugs that came off the ships from the Far East were who was responsible. Fleas had infested the rats - only the rats did not die from the fleas, like we did. We walloped the rats with broom handles and anything we could find to kill them dead - and for all our efforts we were only killing the messenger. The bludgeoned rats' bodies went cold and then the living bugs jumped off their hides and onto us, the warmer hosts.

I told the rats I knew that already. I wanted something from them I did not know.

That's when they told me rats are a single community, they are one big universal colony, a single organism, and a swarm bigger than bees - what one rat knows, all rats will know. What one rat can adapt to - all rats adapt to. They have a universal pack collective conscious and unconscious. They are one smart swarm, rats are.

They waxed on about how they appreciated my being empathetic towards them. So, it was not merely my looks which attracted them to me. It was also by reason of my sensitive and compassionate ways. What I am saying is: Because of my nature, they thought there was something I could do for them.

At first, I was a bit nervous. Maybe there was a slight premonition of a slippery slope here. I had this sense they wanted something from me that would be...would be like selling guns to the Indians. Something like that. Something which might put me in a bad light, later on.

I told them of my misgivings.

In response, they said they knew I was an authority on all those experiments done on rats and they emphasized my being simpatico to them...and I said, yes, that was true...and they...and they said they were as interested in my well-being as I was in theirs. ...Oh, this was after several months of chatter. Then one night, they asked me to follow them - and they took me to a very special rat. A rat named Plato.

Plato lived three levels below in an old abandoned subway stop. It was down there my life took a different course, one from which I could never return.

Plato looked and acted like all the others; except he carried a little stick around with him. He used it like a cane, or a staff. He was the only rat I ever saw handle a piece of wood in any way at all, come to think of it. He must have learned it in some experiment. He could lean on it. Twirl it. He could point it at you when he wanted to make a point. For some reason Plato was their spokesman, or spokes-rat, I guess you would say. It was easier for me to talk man-to-rat with him than it was for me to talk to all of the others at the same time. In the early days I never was certain if they truly had a leader, since they all thought as one. Nonetheless, it was through Plato I made my deal and it was through him I was paid my reward.

Plato asked me if I could share with them the results of the body of tests mankind had done on rats. Could I find out how the rats scored and tested out on the vast body of experiments done on them? The rats meant no harm to us, he said. He emphasized how the results from these scientific works could be of great use to them. After all, the rats had already paid for the studies with their lives.

So, I agreed to be of assistance; for the sake of the colony, for my new friends. I told them it would take a great deal of my time to do this, but it was something I could do. Yes, I could create my own Ratsileaks.

Plato told me the swarm knew about our system of money. Rats had been watching us for centuries and they had learned of our ways. So then, as a reward for my good work on their behalf, they would bring me money and jewelry and all sorts of lost valuables. And they could, and they did, and I thrived, and - well, you cannot blame only the rats for what happened.

End of Chapter 1

Postscript to Chapter 1

SPOILER ALERT: The Rats have already won. It was a slam dunk. The problem is, it was not a game - and the Rats are not playing around. ...Unfortunately, that is the good news.

If you are among the rising number who think current events, large and small, are not going quite right, yet you still hope for a meaningful life, then my tale will be of ultimate concern to you.

My suggestion to you is to put all other matters aside and read the rest of my Papers *toute suite*. Pay no mind to the possibility this document you are holding in your hands should be 'classified' information. The odds are you cannot be held liable for looking at them. Most likely, no one will ever even find out you have seen this material – shameful as much of it is.

I was extremely fortunate to make a getaway from my interrogators and be able to return to leak…no, make that: *pour* out the facts to you. If only you will pay attention. Perhaps, we will meet someday, but if not: May the Rats enjoy your smell and may they be generous to you, with you – whatever.

<u>"Able"</u>

Say "Hello" to Able. He lives in the Sub-basement of the Plaza Hotel. Right now, he is deciding whether he will skitter over to the Hotel's kitchen, or treat himself to one of Room Service's food pantries. Life's been good to Able, and it's about to get a whole lot better.

CHAPTER 2

OBSCURITY

... (Two years have passed since our story began.)

Much data, much knowledge has been accumulated for the rats, thanks to me. I should say: I assembled more information regarding scientific experiments on rats than exists in any other repository in the world. Not only have I compiled it - but the rats and I are analyzing the collective studies and we know how to use the information more effectively than does mankind. You should understand, the acquisition of information by humans is used competitively and for profit - and, thus, not shared for the good of all. Unless there is some sort of monetary advantage to giving away good knowledge from one group of humans to another, it is rarely done. Rats share everything, freely - pretty near. But we'll get to that later.

The rats have paid me well for my contribution. I am rich, rich, rich, close to becoming a 'One-Percenter'. Rare coins, fabulous jewels, and bearer bonds kept flowing in. Every day valuable assets were deposited through my threshold's trap door; usually in the early morning hours. I soon had to establish a network of auction houses, pawnbrokers, and fences to convert my newly found assets to deposit-able currency. I became a fixture at the Diamond district on 47th Street, where I unloaded the best of gems. It was well worth the effort. As far as gathering and analyzing information goes, I could live anywhere; it was the asset conversion process which necessitated my living in Manhattan.

Soon, I had enough liquidity to purchase one of the larger apartments at the Plaza Hotel. Talk about upgrade in lifestyle! You know the Plaza.

It is where Eloise, the six-year old scamp of literary fame is said to have walked the halls. Her portrait hangs on a lobby wall near the Palm Court. The apartments are very nice, I must say. And they are readily accessible to the rats, who have been running wild in the Plaza for well over a century. The rats know every nook and cranny of the place. They were the ones who suggested I move there.

Soon after I moved in, the rats advised me to contribute to a charitable cause. So, I built a geriatric ward in Mount Sinai. (I'll tell you more about that later, when it becomes absolutely necessary to introduce my mother to you. Mom being such a disappointing figure in my life, I bring her up as infrequently as possible.)

The Plaza was most convenient for them and for me - since, after I moved in I learned about a certain rat named Bacci who lived in the lower basement. Bacci was soon to become an important player in my life.

The lower sub-basements had been closed off by hotel management over fifty years ago - due to the uncontrollable rat infestation. The decision had been to simply seal off the nether regions - in sort of a détente maneuver. Time passed, and Bacci moved in, as legend has it.

Remember Plato? I told you I had suspected he might not have been their supreme *leader*. Well, my first instinct was right. Plato, who was ageing before my very eyes, was a big deal, yes, but he merely filled roles of ambassador and recruiter. It was only after I had delivered many reams of solid information to him did he introduce me to Bacci. When I first entered Bacci's realm, Plato feebly left the room by backing away from her and not looking directly into her eyes. I noticed that. I took to noticing a lot in those days. One, because everything was so new to me and: Two, I was not sure of the ground upon which I was standing. Now, nothing is new - and I know what I am standing on.

By reading this, you are among the first to know about Bacci. For no one has revealed Bacci's existence and early whereabouts until I have done by this treacherous (or redeeming) act of releasing this tale. Bacci lived, conveniently, twelve stories below me - in total obscurity, as far as humans were concerned. She reigned in a cavernous room known only to a small handful of human recruits. The truth is I do not know how many inductees there were at that time. (The rats had given us a nickname, which sounds something like 'Chumpers.') But in relation to our human population of seven billion-plus people, we 'Chumpers' were, and still are, a small handful.

Bacci was the chosen rat, the one all others adore. They worship her and they would kill for her; but more of that later. For now, let me tell you Bacci was like no other rat, but at the same time she could only be a rat. It is said she was slow to rage but quick to temper. Rumor had it Bacci could not die, but you know what rumors are worth – and rumors abound - and we will see. Much is said, little is known. She ate and digested my rat's study data like so much smelly, rotting pieces of food waste garbage and then she somehow regurgitated the end knowledge of all those studies to her swarm. And what Bacci knew, or wanted them to know, they all know; and I am left with a new Rolex and a pearl necklace for my labors.

Now for the others, the other Chumpers. I was perhaps the first, but certainly not the last to serve. Among their enlistments, Plato had signed up: Lobbyists, Senators, Congressmen, police-chiefs... even a former President of the United States is on the payroll. Yes. They all had their reasons for signing up, some of them good, I like to think. Like what? You ask. Answer: Family needs. Pay off debts...you know the drill. But, whatever, we all gained great wealth as a reward. To sop up our guilt for allying with rodents and serving their needs - and gaining financial independence thereby, we have joined among the great names in charity givers. We give to good causes: Church Bazaars, Politicians, College scholarships. Me? Remember, the ward I donated at Mount Sinai? For all the money I have given them, they let my mother live there. She has her own private room. It is a nice thing for a son to do for his mother. I go to her room almost every night. As I've said, I'll tell you more about her and those trips later.

The point is: Though we Chumpers give Charity Balls, and we sponsor summer camps for sick children, and we finance Public Radio and on and on; we take our coin from the rats - and deep down we all know what we are. We know.

It is reasonable to ask: "Why?" Why all this recruiting of the Chumpers? What was this all about? There was something more than the gathering of the results of Man/Rat studies. What was going on? What could all those other Chumpers do for them? One eventually had to ask. "*HHHmmm,*" I thought.

It took me quite a while after I was 'all in', so to speak, but I finally worried out the bigger picture:

The rats depend upon our waste for their thriving. That is the sum of it. You see, in the Swarm's mind, <u>the primary purpose of man is to provide the rats with sustenance: Man's role in nature is to produce the very diet of the Swarm</u> - to provide the good rat life. And the rats have long been concerned we are fouling the nest, to mix a metaphor. (I do not have time to tweak my message to you in finicky, edit-y, literary fashion. It would be best if you were to focus on *what* I am saying to you - and not worry about *how* I am saying it - nor should you be distracted by the fact that I have been a traitor to the human race. However, I am sure many of you will take me for my word, simply because you know me to be rich and I know how you value that. The rats, too, realize how much you value the opinions of the rich. They can play that fiddle well. Be advised.)

Where was I? ... Oh, yes. Bacci. Maybe I should tell you about Bacci and the Big Inaugural Dinner in the Plaza's sub-sub-basement.

It was more than a year ago, a hot August night – it must have been over ninety outside. But down there it was a chilly fifty degrees. Rats like it cool. They cannot bear the heat. Too much heat makes them drool and spastically roll over on their backs. (They hate the fact we are heating up the planet. Remember that.) In the far end of the room there were thousands of rats, all eating God knows what it was that was molding and putrefying in a large disgusting pile. In the center of the room was Bacci herself. None of the other rats dared look directly at her, in fear of becoming locked into those red, huge, yet beady eyes. In the Chumpers' end of the room, at a long banquet table there were about fifty of us - uncomfortably sitting stone still, not talking to each other. Not looking into one another's eyes.

Bacci was enormous. Perhaps the biggest rat ever. Even bigger than the biggest of the big rats of the freezing Pleistocene epoch. Some said her frame and girth were the result of an experiment where she was force fed next to a nuclear drainpipe. But this detail has not been certified. She sported a pink name tag which had 'Bacci' written in it. The tag was a bit ragged. It must have been attached to her by some research assistant - as a lab-rat identifier. By the time I saw it, one end of the label had grown into her hide, near the back of her neck. It looked like it could not be removed. I think Bacci wore it as some perverse badge of honor.

Overhead, high on a back wall, Bacci had somehow managed to get a Chumper to place a big, antique looking, wreck of a sign which read, "In Obscuritas, Securitas Est". I suspected this credo had some portent, but the meaning of which I could not fathom at the time. As for us, the august body of humans gathered there, we were all dressed to the nines. Each Chumper sitting in front of a disgusting pile of rotting fruit rinds and slimy vegetable leaves. Bacci commanded us to eat - and we ate. Even the former President of the United States ate ...and Bacci was merry, for she knew us well - and she disliked us. Alongside of our dirty bowls of degenerating food, each of one us had been given several little party favors, such as: Gold fillings and expensive old watch bands – gleaned from God knows where. Ahh, yes. What a night it was. Before dessert, Bacci spoke.

And she spoke words of foreboding, words which will forever be etched in my mind; but forever won't be long from now; unless you heed my words.

End of Chapter 2

<u>"Tulip"</u>

"Whoa!" Says Tulip. "Those Chumpers can really eat. I'm so hungry I could eat a pile of compost. Maybe, I'll crawl on the table and grab a bite.

CHAPTER 3

LIGHTER

If this were a novel, or a movie, you would have already been introduced to the romantic interest. A beautiful, tattooed, blond would have been thunderstruck by my machismo ways and the two of us would be fighting against the injustices of the world. But this is neither a novel, nor a movie. No such luck for you, or for my agent.

However, rats are equal opportunity creatures. And there were female Chumpers from the start. The first one I knew of was named Candy. She was not destined to be my romantic interest. By the time I met her - saw her - would be a better way of putting it, she was seated in a stupefied trance. She had a carbo-shocked thousand-yard stare and anyone with half a brain could see she was non-compos-mentis.

Candy was placed across the table from me and about two spaces over to my left. She sat perfectly straight and stared at her plate through the whole rotting meal. She seemed to have been given a special meal, for it looked different than ours, bready stuff mostly – un-identifiable and unattractive to my palette. When she ate, she did it with perfect Miss Manners' form: Correct usage of the knife, proper fork selection - no fingering with the food, employing the napkin to gently wipe away the little bubble of grease that dripped off something which might have been a jellyfish tentacle. I hear those gooey, stringy things can be a delicacy - but not so when served up by Bacci. Anyway, Candy...

I knew her name because we were all obliged to wear name tags, first name only. We had been given code names by the rats. My first thought about the name tags was they were a sort of 'turn-about is fair play' game of Bacci's, because of her own ingrown marker. And that might have been the case because rats enjoy tricky, covert subterfuges. Secret, sneaky stuff. It seemed sort of military straight to them, as well as adding a bit of rat whimsy to the whole affair. The code names they gave us made more sense to them then did our birth names. What did they know about our Saints, or heroes or whoever we are named after? It was by these nicknames we Chumpers were to refer to each other. Our past names were of the past. Like a witness protection program of some sort. Candy was so named, I guess, because of her predilection for food. Me? They code-named me Benedict. These secret and fun names were not as true an identifier to the rats as were our individual smells. We all seem pretty much the same to them, except for our particular aromas. On our tags, under our names, we all had a little, smelly, brownish schmear. The rats claimed they could distinguish us by virtue of sniffing out our vices. Can you imagine such a thing? Basically, our smells go in seven different groups. They believed they could sniff out: Greed, Lust, Anger, and so on. The rats picked up this knowledge from a study our scientists did on them, in which they hoped to learn how to control behavior through understanding pheromones. Sometimes, we are too clever for our own good. These studies were shelved because the scientists could not figure out how to make money out of their conclusions. But the rats, not caring about profits, figured out how to use the results. So, those tags had little stinky bits of those attributes smudged unto our name-pieces. I have often wondered what comprised my unique scent. Most the time, I think I am pretty much smell free. At least no one ever told me I had a bad body odor, except my mom. But she was outright mean, so I don't take what she had to say about my smell personally.

... Anyway, as I was saying, Candy was a Chumper and what she contributed to the party was: Herself. Yes: Herself. While I was paid for providing information by gathering data, Candy was paid for the information she gave them by allowing the rats to experiment upon her. Remember the study I told you about, the one where scientists made a young rat fat and then dieted it down and then it gained weight again? Remember that one? Well, Candy was in the second weight gaining phase of a variation on that study. She was already done with the experiment where they moved her cheese, metaphorically speaking, and she was in the process of going quite mad, actually speaking. You see, the rats were conducting some of the same experiments on us that we have been doing to them. What goes around, comes around, I guess. Candy was a groundbreaking lab human. Don't laugh, it could happen to you.

Word has it we humans respond to experiments regarding pain, addiction, disease, etc., roughly in the same manner as do the rats. Candy being the first of the homo-sapiens, to be subjected to - make that: *pioneer* these studies for the Rodentia, does deserve some recognition. I hear she is extraordinarily wealthy - although, she does not know it. She is a glazed blob of human flesh, perhaps fit only to ingest and excrete. At least they paid her. When humans are finished with their experiments, we simply throw the rats away. The rats never throw us away, as long as we can make garbage. I may have been the uber-Julian Assange of my time; but Candy was the game changer, for through her the rats realized they could not only learn from our studies; they could alter our behavior. They could make us fat and sluggish, if need be. Why, they could make us hit the bar for more drugs, could they not? What next did these studies promise? Thanks, Candy.

So, where was I? Oh, yes: The after-dinner speech.

Bacci, who was huge, she must have weighed weigh over a hundred pounds. She had shoulders. You will note most rats do not have shoulders. And she had a thick neck. The big creature was different than the others; but very much a rat at the same time. Maybe, she was a heralding of rats to come. Who knows?

Bacci did a repulsive dance for the benefit of all attending. The wildly feeding and overtly breeding regular ground troop rats went berserk with joy. Bacci hopped around and swished her tail about like it was some sort of water snake and squealed and she made thrusts and quivered as if in sexual delight. The huge beast turned in quick tight circles and even rolled over several times. Something about it made me both nauseous and fearful. When she was finished with her little entertainment, she turned to the Chumpers' table and spoke - and to make certain we all understood her every word she used me as her simultaneous translator.

(Narrator's note: All Chumpers are given rodent language lessons, a Ratsetta Course – which, I am proud to say, I created. I also wrote and developed the software for a phone app which speaks either language upon request. The app will be available through one of our major telecoms soon – but that is neither here nor there. Bacci, not being certain all the Chumpers were fully up to speed by the time of the Big Dinner, insisted I do the voice-over – to be sure everybody got the message loud and clear.)

Through me she said:

"You may wonder why you are here tonight. Cheek, Cheek." (She made these guttural, yet squeaky noises which gave an annoyingly, disturbing cadence to her delivery.) "...*We* want to thank you for what you have done for us. Now *we* need you to know exactly what you are. Cheek, cheek." The other rats paid no attention to Bacci at this time - as they were busy propagating their kind. Bacci stared out over our heads as if we were not worthy of her glare. Her red eyes seeming to cast laser like beams across the room. She continued:

"Tonight, *We* announce the beginning of the end of the Dominion of the Homo sapiens. Yes. Cheek, cheek. Your species has been here for how long? Millions of years? Or sixty-six hundred years. You cannot even agree on how long you have been here. Yet you dominate. And you fight each other. You run riot over the earth as if it were your playground. Cheek. Cheek.

"...Records show since the inception of life on this earth, there have been *five great extinctions of species* – over many millions of years. It took asteroids, volcanic eruptions –huge catastrophic and cataclysmic events to cause these extinctions..." (Bacci has boned up on the subject, you have to admit.) "...and you Homo sapiens, cheek, you are causing the Sixth Extinction - or, as I call it, 'The Pathetic Extinction' of species with your recklessness. You pollute the land, water and air. You do this in the name of your economics or your gods...and claim it is your right as superior creatures. Anything for man, you say. *You* are the *calamitous* event of our time." She paused, and then added, dramatically, "We say: 'No more! No more of *anything and everything for man*'! Cheek. Cheek."

Bacci went on about how the rats depended upon man for food...and how that had been an agreeable arrangement for eons - but things have changed and man has lost balance and even the rats were getting sick from man's effluents and chemicalized pollutants and so on and on with all that political crap you would expect to hear from liberal bottom of the heap 99 per centers - but not from a disgusting one hundred pound mutated rat.

To quote her some more: (You may have noticed Bacci referred to herself in the third person singular – as if she were a queen or something – or in the third person plural, or third rat singular and plural, or whatever it is. It is an intimidating approach to public speaking, I think.) "After all this time of Homo sapiens rule, man does not even know how much to eat, or what to eat. He does not know if it is getting colder or hotter. He knows *nothing* after all these years, and now he is threatening the very existence of his own species with his weapons of anti-god-particle mass and massive destruction. Bacci cannot have that. And Bacci has learned that man, who cannot feed himself without becoming obese, and cannot feed all seven billion plus of his population, has turned to eating rats in various parts of the world. Cheek, Cheek! ***Rats!*** Mind you! In India, Thailand, Africa, Vietnam. Rats are being eaten both as sustenance and as a delicacy..."

At this point I heard one of our fellow Chumpers make a contemptuous chuckle, and then a little louder than under his besotted breath, "Of all the stupid, filthy, low down crap..."

...Bacci, seeming to take no notice, continued with threatening authority, "If this trend continues...Well, it won't. Cheek. Cheek."

"*HHHmmm*", I started to think.

So, it came to pass, Bacci informed us we will aid her in recruiting more of us. The powerful among us will push through legislation which will help Big Pharma and Big Agra to supply the food and medicinal chain with substances which will make us fat, make us mentally numb, and make us live long and useless lives, capable of only producing low level, low tech garbage. She said the Chumpers would help her because we want to remain rich and if we would not, then ... then we could not be trusted, like the fellow at the end of the table cannot be trusted. And we all looked over at the formerly disgruntled, recently sneering Senator who had snorted at Bacci's words. His face had fallen onto his plate from what had obviously been an ingestion of a meal suddenly gone bad.

How did she do that so quickly? I wondered. I had read the Russians were pretty good at that kind of thing - but it looked like Bacci and her crew had perfected the act. We were riveted to our seats; I can tell you that.

I suspected Bacci had much more to say; but she interrupted herself and said "Oh, Cheek. Cheek. Look what I have learned to do. I learned this from some of the military experiments you have been conducting in Zone 9 out West...:" and then Bacci stopped making any sound and ceased all visible motion. The room went silent, and slowly...she began to hover. Yes, hover, maybe twelve feet in the air. She was lighter than air, this one gigantic, mutated rat, defying gravity. She floated directly over our heads, like a living drone. I have been to Vegas and I have seen the best – but I have never witnessed a hovering act like this one. No strings, no mirrors – just a one-hundred-pound rat floating in mid-air. David Copperfield would eat his heart out to find out how she did it. There was not a sound in the room, except for a slurping noise from Candy who was sucking on a chicken bone. The rats had stopped doing whatever they were doing, and they marveled in awe. *'Oh, My God!'* I remember thinking. *'I am on the right side of events.'*

It was then I knew they could do whatever they wanted - unless the humans got their act together very soon.

Dinner was not over. There was more.

End of Chapter 3

"Vinnie"

Vinnie is a careful fellow. You can see him quietly staring at a group of Humans – from a social distance, wondering if they are safe to be around, wondering if they are 'True Chumpers'. Some of the humans don't smell quite right.

CHAPTER 4

WORD

None of the Chumpers had much of an appetite left for dessert, except for Candy, who was eating like a Millennial.

However, Bacci was not sensitive to our mood and it was over a coagulating, melted ice cream of unidentified flavors, when she took the opportunity to introduce us to our new cadre of Leads.

Plato was dead by now and we needed to establish new relationships with our fellow rats. Rats typically live to be about eighteen months. So, there is a constant changing of the guard. Fresh new faces, if you will. We Chumpers were always putting on our best smiley faces for them – and sprucing up our body odors as much as possible. It was as if we were perpetually applying for the job. Talk about stress.

The interesting thing is: Rats are quicker to adapt - in many ways - than are we. Studies prove it. Consider how long it takes us to train an army in a foreign land. Years it takes. For example, it required over a decade for us to train the Afghans to our fighting ways - and they have been warriors for God knows how long. We coach our fellow humans on how to make war, and often, our valiant efforts do not take hold. And worse, upon occasion, some of us turn around and shoot our own trainers. No control. No knowing what is coming next with the Homo Sapiens. Not the case with the rats, they being a progressive swarm and all. It seems we humans have to keep learning the same lesson over and over again - if we learn it at all. What I want to impart to you here is our new rat contacts were fully up to speed on each new Chumper at first sight - though *we* had to get to know each new rat we were to deal with from square one. We were not trading on any kind of equal footing. Have you ever tried to get a job through a human resource guy, and he had your resume in front of him and you did not know who the heck you were talking to? You did not know how to play the guy - and he knew what size underwear you wear, and how bad you did in trigonometry. Well, it was like that – except the human resource guy in our case was a rat

Bacci told us she had important work ahead of her and would not be readily available to us in the future. We were thus to be relegated to her supreme assistant; a rat named Mose. And then she, hovering over our heads, commanded Mose to come out.

Suddenly, and without any drum roll or show of pomp, a grey rat, about twelve inches from head to the beginning of the tail, and carrying the typical rat weight of about one pound, crawled over the slumping body of our recently departed Senator - and onto the center of the Chumpers' table. This was Mose. Immediately behind Mose came strutting another rat, who looked quite unlike the dignified Mose.

Once you spend a little time with rats, you will note they do not all look alike. They are as different from each other as are we to one another. This other rat was jet black, and smaller than your average rat. He was appreciably smaller than Mose, maybe carrying six ounces all told - but you could tell he was fully grown. Must have been a runt. A runt rat with a Napoleonic complex. To my disgust, he had human-like thumbs opposing his fore-claws. He must have been the consequence of a rat genetic experiment our scientists had been conducting in a medical laboratory. Other than the thumbs, to me, he still looked like a rat, though a diminutive one. His name was: Err. Just to look at him, you knew he was trouble on the rise. He was probably full of neurotic impulses due to his formative months at the hands of the experimenters. In all my searches, I never came across humans doing any rat therapy or post traumatic work on lab animals. Looking at Err's thumbs, it did not take any brains to realize Err was the raw, unvarnished consequence of our past doings. "*HHHmmm.*"

Bacci, looked down upon our table, signaled for Mose to take over and then she, making a few of those "Cheek, cheek" noises of hers, slowly turned in mid-air and floated for the exit. That was the last I ever saw of

her. As she made her graceful departure every rat in the room watched in
awe – as did we

Chumpers. Awe, as a topic is important - and we will come back to
that feature later.

Back to Mose & Err.

Mose assumed the rodent's authority posture in that he was perched
up on his back haunches, with his front claw-like paws resting near chest
high, pointing forward. He remained there, never speaking a word -
looking around at our attentive assemblage. Finally, Err spoke. Err spoke
for Mose. It was as if we were not worthy enough for someone of Mose's
stature to speak directly to us. Insulting, in a way. Sort of putting us in our
proper place in the hierarchy in the room. *Maybe he is a mute,* I remember
thinking, hopefully. "*HHHmmm.*"

Despite his puny size, Err was one scary looking rat. I'd equate him
to the Goebbels of Rats, if you would like a point of reference. He spoke
perfect English, which I found disconcerting. Probably the result of
another one of those dreadful lab-experiments. If they came out with a
pill you could take so you could speak another language, then it might
have been worth what went on with the rats in the basements – but I have
not heard of such, yet. Have you? Personally, I find it is far preferable to
have invaders come to your land and speak in their own language, than
it is to have them come in and speak your language better than you do.
Err's being so articulate in our tongue helped remove any dash of a hope
I might have had thinking we were superior to these creatures. When he
spoke, we had already lost Round One.

Came now the *Grand Finale* of the evening, if the hovering gig did
not knock you out:

Without any adieu, Err speaking for Mose, made a few opening
comments which were meant to show much rat wisdom. Err bowed toward
Mose, pointed one of his revolting thumbs at him and the other thumb at
us, and rattled off a few mothers of pearl. Here are a few samples:

- "Garbage of the rich is no different than the garbage of the
  poor." And...
- "The food you will eat will be better for you than it tastes." (I took
  this as a foreboding.) And...

- "Tasers are more effective than cattle prods." (Another warning of some sort, to be fully understood at a future date.)

Err went on and on like this for a few minutes. As you will learn, the above gems were not from the wit and wisdom of Mose & Err; but were distilled lifts from a rat far greater than they.

Mose continued to stare silently over the heads of the Chumpers. Then Err, delivered the evening's main message. He summed up a big picture scenario for us. It was comprised of a recapitulation of history as seen by the rats with a slice of Newer Age (or, as I name it: "Sewer Age") spiritual meanderings.

Surprise. Surprise. It turns out these two rats were on to religion. Yes, they had observed in the Rat/Man studies that man, throughout his life's span, had mobilized and survived better than most species because of the assistance he received from the mere holding on to his various religious beliefs; whatever they were. According to the rat version of our history, man had accomplished great land expansions, the conquering of one another, his enslavements, his resource acquisitions, every form of hegemony and domination in the name of - and with the motivating blessings of his self-imposed gods. Man's gods had inspired him to do what he always wanted and intended to do in the first place - so said Mose & Err. And the various gods had given man 'Divine Commandments' in order that he would behave and fulfill his natural role in a Grand Scheme. But man, (according to the First Speech Upon the Chumpers' Table; Book of Mose, Chapter 1, Verse 3-12) has gone off his ordained path – and, therefore, the old Ten Commandments no longer worked. They were not good enough, in the context of our present times. And here was Mose, through the voice of Err, determined to bring to man…if not a new God - a New Order from a New and Better Book. One we could understand. But first, before came the New Order, before anything, there came the new first word in the Better Book. And it was Bad News. Specifically, the new first Word was: "OBEY"

And then came a new second Word. And the new second Word was: "US"

If you put the two new words together, you got: "OBEY US." With an exclamation point at the end!

… "Cheek."

The party was over.

End of Chapter 4

"Gloria"

When Gloria watched Bacci that famous night at the Plaza. she was inspired by Bacci's act and has become a block leader Gloria and her pack nibbled away on wires last week, and shut down all the electricity in the 666 Madison Ave. skyscraper. Trump Tower is next on the list.

CHAPTER 5

RED

(And now to live class-lectures taught by Mose & Err...)

Leviticus: 11, 29 forbade the eating of rats. It's true. I looked it up. Mose & Err were right. No eating of rats. God said. Unfortunately, I fell for that old trick of when an authority figure bolts out of the chute with fact after provable fact - one just caves in and assumes the speaker has everything right after that. Next thing you know, you have succumbed to the whole megillah being offered up - and then it is down the old rat hole. Watch out for facts, is all I can say.

Mose & Err were as outraged as was Bacci that humans in various parts of the world had taken anew to eating rats. The very wealthy and the lower ninety-nine per cent were behaving poorly. This had to stop. Everybody in my classroom agreed whole heartedly, our heads bobbing in accord.

Obviously, nobody heeded Leviticus anymore. Those who were still following Scripture were thumbing mostly through the New Testaments - and soon that will fall out of favor.

Mose & Err were so livid over this rat eating business, it was as if they were implying we should go back to the 'Eye for an Eye' type justice, only it had more of the tone of a 'Whole body for an Eye' type justice, if you

27

take my meaning. I did not raise my hand to ask where this was going. I thought better than to ask questions.

• •

I will interrupt myself in the telling of this story - just this once - to respond to a question put to me by my editor. She will be replaced if I detect her questions come from a place of disbelief, for we have no time for that. The question she asked was: "How did anybody see anything in the sub-sub-basement of the Plaza? Obviously, the Plaza did not furnish lighting for the event. It must have been pitch-black down there."

No, the Plaza did not do the lighting. The rats recruited Chumpers who were electricians. Duh. Granted, you might think electricians make enough without having to betray their own kind. Deep down electricians are no different than Congressmen, Lobbyists, Lawyers, Information Technologists, Dentists, and Contract Mercenaries. They are all the same. Everybody wants more and there is never enough. We all know that.

Take it from me, the place was well lit. And the sound system was top of the line. So, do not waste our time with more stupid, doubting or cleverly crafted questions. They will only serve to get you off on a tangent and while you are off on a tangent, you will miss the point.

Back to the classroom.

• •

Mose & Err held many classes for the troops during the first few months of 'The Reign of The Teacher'. We New York City Chumpers were now about fifty in number, but our numbers were growing daily by one-zies and two-zies. A sprinkling of the elderly started to come in. Makes sense when you think of it. Working for the rats when you were over sixty was far better than waiting for your deflating social security check. Better than trading down from a house to a trailer looking for a shuffle-board court, with the only hope is maybe you will get a nurse who will be gentle with you when he flips you over. And young adults joined too, what with college debts and no way to pay them off, living with their parents, who were not having much fun with the new American family forever get-togethers. Yes, the rats had no trouble acquiring recruits. All races were accepting the call early on. A rich mosaic, or rainbow, or whatever you'd want to call it. The pot was melting, that is for sure.

One night, before one of Mose & Err's mandatory classes, I met a man who had come down from the Upper West Side. Imagine that. Turns out we Chumpers in The Plaza were the tap root Chapter. There were already budding cells of Chumpers and their cohorts sprouting up all over the U.S.A. It was, and is, the best kept secret in town – probably helped by the fact that people really do not want to know what is really going on, even if it is going on right beneath their feet. An insurgent, revolutionary movement hiding in plain sight. Do not tell me there is no such thing as a conspiracy. Tell that to Julius Caesar. Tell that to JFK. Tell it to the Climate Change Deniers. ...And now we have this.

If a Chumper were thought of highly enough, soon, he could go just about anywhere. There was a Chapter forming on the Upper West Side – under the ground floor of Zabars' Delicatessen. And another Chapter down on Wall and Broadway, under the Trinity Church graveyard. Bacci attended meetings at all locations. I was told she was always showing off with her scary hovering thing.

The network was growing. And I say this with pride: I was in the Alpha Chapter. And I was Chumper #1. That is saying something.

But I am wandering off point.

There was only one Mose & Err, though, and all the Teachers out in the Provinces were to teach the Word of Mose & Err; for Mose & Err were thought to be connected to a higher power and were channeling accordingly.

The reason for the lectures was to properly disinform us and then have us join in on their plan with a full enthusiastic lather.

I thought there was no such word as "disinform", thinking it was the kind of word which was concocted by an inarticulate President we had a few years ago - but I looked it up – and there it was. Disinform is exactly what the rats wanted to do to us; alter whatever knowledge we had in our brains, re-program our acculturation - and infuse us with new confirmations – which would fire up urges in us, designed to satisfy their own purposes. This was more sophisticated than mere propaganda.

The plan was to get the Chumpers to swallow the New Ordeal, digest it and then have them collaborate as leaders and inspire the rest of the humans with the ordained morality of the Neo-New Age.

The Judeo-Christian Ten Commandments were altered to accommodate this scheme. Some of the old ones were gone completely. There were some newly fangled and added to the list. The updated Commandments were not hurled to us all at once. They did not come in nice chiseled tablets. Oh, no. They came in repetitive lectures. Two Commandments at a time. The rats had learned from Man/Rat studies that man learns most optimally when only two messages were offered up in a given lecture. Two of anything is all man's tiny brain (in relation to his body mass) can absorb. I will go over the first two with you:

Lesson #1

Right off the bat, Mose & Err eliminated the 'Thou shalt not steal' biggie. Err spoke the words for Mose: "Man steals. He cannot stop himself. ...Look at corruption, which, perhaps, accounts for one third of the world's economy. ...Look at the daily police blotters. ... Look at all the security in place to try to prevent theft. Stealing trumps all preventative measures. ...Yet security is perhaps the biggest industry known to man: Locks, doors, hide-aways, banks, bodyguards, border-guards, police, cameras, passwords – on and on. The theft which goes on between you is without bounds. This is a Commandment which has not and cannot be obeyed. Therefore, it is useless and unenforceable. More ridiculous than your Prohibition Experiment. ...Thus, we forbid the teaching of 'Do not steal'."

If that were not enough, Err beat up on the point some more. "Stealing from one another is the very essence of, the backbone of, the great job creator of - and a vital part of man's economic survival ...and must continue unabated and with resolve. You, Chumpers, are yourselves the beneficiaries of thievery for we not only scavenge for your treasure, we steal it and you know this. So, no more with the 'Thou shalt not steal' noise." *HHHmmm*, I thought, easy for the rats to say, since there is nothing we would want to steal from them. Next came:

Lesson #2:

This tutorial was concerned with coveting thy neighbor's goods. It turns out it is O.K. to do that – coveting is what makes the human' world turn, sayeth the speaking rat. Man cannot help himself here, anyway – as it is his nature to want what others have. So, go ahead with the nature thing. Want what you will, take what you want. No god worth its salt would create you, beloved creatures, to be one way and then forbid you to be what you are.

Made sense, when you thought about it. Again, the thought drilled into us repeatedly during the early Elimination of the Commandments Lectures was: Coveting leads to theft and vice-versa and forget about them as no-no's forbidden from up above. Over and over with this. Just as I was about to bang my forehead to pulp on the table from the tedious boredom of it all, Mose & Err introduced us to the First Chumpers' Teaching Assistant. Her name was Red. She was the most beautiful creature I had ever seen.

I was pretty sure she was human.

End of Chapter 5

"Thelma & Louie"

Thelma says to Louie, "Let's go to Bloomingdales and watch the women scream and go crazy when they see us. Louie, always accommodating, says, "Count me in!"

CHAPTER 6

PREHISTORIC

'RED' was the moniker printed on the Rat-tag which was affixed to her bustier. To make certain we knew her identifier markings, and that she was proud of them, she had RED tattooed in crimson bold over her right breast. The smell patch smeared on to her nameplate is associated with the vice of rage and the archaic fault described in Proverbs: "Him that soweth discord". Apparently, the God of the old Good Book, "...detesteth *him* that soweth discord" and termed such 'an anathema' - but Red was a *her*, maybe that is what made her so mad. Whatever it was - she was capable of sowing discord. Those who have smelled her up close agree with me she has an intoxicating aroma - and it drives them crazy. Stay away from Red if you are an average human - is my message to you.

Red was perfect, up there on that stage. Perfect physically; but physicality isn't everything, is it? I mean anyone who could do what she does for a living has got to be seriously flawed. No?

She looked as if she were designed, digitally for a super- hero comic book. Strong. She was strong, you could tell. For a nanosecond I had the hope she was going to strut to and fro and carry a placard over her head which would announce the number of the next Commandment Mose & Err was going to talk about. You know, like those babes do at boxing matches. But no, she was above that kind of cheap showgirl pizzazz.

Back and forth like some kind of lioness on the prowl for prey, Red laid claim to the territory of the stage, strolling the entire width of the platform. She looked out over to us, scanning the cluster of Chumpers, her dark green eyes making quick sharp contact with each one in the room.

Her expressionless face never indicating any kind of recognition with us, never revealing what she was thinking or doing up there. But she had to know we were looking at her - and we knew she could care less.

Right down by her ankles, there danced and pranced the cutest little rat you ever saw. Her name was Petal. Petal adored Red. You could tell. She followed Red everywhere in complete and bursting joy. It was a curious counterpoint, visually. My first germ of a thought about this was if that cute little creature could love Red so much - then Red could not be all bad.

Looking at Red stalk about while Err delivered his message, I was reminded of the proctors in high school test rooms. That kind of monitoring always made me feel uneasy – not that I was cheating or anything.

I had long since developed a skill for detecting rat 'tells', and I noticed Red's nose give a slight twitch. Just a twitch - in a trice. And then I heard an almost imperceptible "Cheek". Damned if she couldn't speak rat. I had more than a small twinge of disappointment; realizing I was not the only one in the room who could fluently convers with these creatures. Perhaps, maybe, I was not as unique, as indispensable to them as I had led myself to believe. "*HHHmmm*", I thought, uncomfortably, *Conceivably, I had gotten in over my head.* My next thought was she would be a formidable foe; and in the event that maybe I could not beat her in the hierarchy to come – it might be best if I joined her. I'd have to work on that.

We were in a rat boot camp, mixed with a rat brain washing, blended in with a Rat New Age corporate boondoggle. Some of us were going to come out of it drinking from the fire hose and ready to hit the ground running for the team. And some were not. How was it determined if we failed the camp - did not make the cut? Well, that is where Red came in - she was the decider. She culled out those who were not up to snuff, who was not really buying the program. Remember the Senator who washed out at the Bacci dinner? Bacci had the instinct to smell out weakness and could weed out a dissenter before he could become a problem. She knew who was what. Red had the same skill set.

I guess you could say Red ratted out the defective Chumpers. Red would signal to Err, who was always watching us, and twitch her nose at him and he would twitch something back, and point his grotesque thumbs toward her, as if saying "I got it!" and they'd give a little "Cheek" to one another, as if they were buddies. Err would bow to her in a polite, courtly gesture. Then - at the next session some Chumper would not be in attendance. Red's function was never officially described to us. This is something I observed by watching.

So. To bring you up to speed on our tutorials, let me continue with the new spin on the Old Commandments. To refresh, from the last chapter: It is OK to steal and covet.

Next, we were told we could worship any God we wanted. As far as the rats were concerned, we already did that. Forget about this one. No more pretending. No more of this 'One God Above All' business: Who cares? Believe what you want, but don't force any of your beliefs on each other. Don't fight over this again. Never, ever. Fighting over whose God is best is a big rat 'No-No'. According to the rat's understanding of our religions, many wars have been fought over the God issue and have been responsible for the creation of terrible weapons, some of which are damaging to the earth and consequently to the Rats domain... "... and so, New Rule & Reg # 1: no more wars over God or Gods!" I made like I was taking notes on this one, in case Red was looking at me.

It occurred to me, at this juncture, the rats were sounding a bit like pacifists. I suspected this was not the case; but I had not yet figured out their angle. More was to be revealed on this score, the score of war score.

Go ahead with the, 'gravening of images', or not. No harm either way. Whatever; the rats could care less. Draw Gods, sculpt them. Make candles out of them. "Have fun." No big thing.

As far as oaths, damning, and disrespectful language - we could do as much of that as we wanted to. Rats, themselves, don't swear, curse or use foul language. It has never occurred to them to do so and they do not understand such behavior. But since it seems to relieve tensions in humans, and seeing as it generally lowers the quality of life for people, the rats are happy to let us indulge in this activity.

Forget about honoring the Sabbath. "Which day is that anyway? Is it Saturday? Or Sunday? What? Some god does not want you to work one day, not to make any money? You have to spend time with your family all day and do nothing? Can't even mow the lawn? Just sit around and worship? Cheek? Come on...no one does this anymore. Delete this Commandment". I looked around the room; most heads were nodding in agreement. This is not the stuff of dangerous thought, I thought. We can agree to agree here.

As for "Honor thy father and thy mother," Mose & Err scoffed at this one. Err pontificated on the subject, telling us, "According to your scripture, there was a bargain made here between man and God. It's in the Book. Go to the Googler. Check it out. Cheek. Man was to '… honor thy father and thy mother, that thy days may be long upon the land that the Lord, thy God giveth thee.' …How'd that deal work out for the wannabe long living goody-goody two shoe types who were always so nice to mommy and daddy?"

I did Google it. They were right. You would have thought Mose & Err were priests, or Talmudic scholars, or something. They showed us some of our own studies which proved that honoring mom and dad had nothing to do with longevity in humans. Therefore, we could do as we pleased on this one. "If it is longevity you are after, if you behave according to the New Rules & Regs, you will probably live longer than otherwise," was the new bargain. We all nodded. I continued to take notes. Red looked at someone off to my left and behind me, she sniffed, and her upper lip raised towards a nostril and I saw a pearly white bicuspid - just in a flash of a millisecond this happened. But I saw it and I saw Err do his thumb and bow thing and I bent my head down and took some more notes.

'Bearing false witness' was also of no concern to the rats - and not a required injunction in their New Rules & Regs. They showed us reports which demonstrate that victims of crimes frequently identified the wrong person in line-ups - by 'innocent' mistake. This is caused by our warping and faulty memory facilities. You cannot even trust fingerprinting any longer. It turns out, despite all the scientific methods available; the reading of prints is often artistically (and incorrectly) analyzed. What is false witness anyway? 'Say what you want about who did what; false is as good as true,' so spoke our rodent guru, (giving meaning the expression 'lying rat', I suppose.)

I was beginning to get the message, the big picture. The dawn was flowing slowly, but I finally saw the dim light during the next lecture. I am talking about the last Commandment to be mutilated.

It was the one which admonishes: "Thou shalt not kill." Err said we no longer have to obey this one. He went on with a rant about how we all kill each other anyway and how we should stop tormenting ourselves over this. I mean if you took him at his word, you would have to be ga-ga. At first, I thought I was missing some sort of a metaphor.

It took this last lecture on the Commandments to confirm my suspicions of what the rats were up to. Let's see if you are up to speed. Think. What did the rats really truly, madly, deeply want?

Remember, "No more Wars in the name of God"? And Mose & Err saying we can murder? Yes. Murder was fine and to be encouraged. How does the one jibe with the other? I did not raise my hand and ask. But in a flash of intuitive insight I saw the rats wanted to teach man how to go forth and bring chaos, low-tech chaos, into the world. Originally, the Big Ten were handed down so we could behave and organize and thrive - in an orderly 'civilized' fashion. As far as the Rats were concerned: Chaos was good.

However, murder, in the name of war, led to Big War with nuclear, chemical and biological tailings. This was the direction man was headed towards, with momentum – and it is intolerable. The rats wanted us to go back, back to our prehistoric lives. Their vision was a sort of post-Apocalyptic world - without having to have the Apocalypse; an event many human believers long for. The rats simply did not want us to poison the nest or blow the whole place up. I could live with that.

End of Chapter 6

<u>"Petal"</u>

Petal, the world's cutest rat. Don't you agree?

CHAPTER 7

AUDACIOUS

"So much information, so little knowledge."
-Excerpted from: Mathuzala's article in https://
notesfromtheroomofwonder.com

∙∙

The situation became fluid and the river of events rose high and moved at flood speed. So, put down your cellphone, turn off your screens and listen up because a lot happens at the same time and it is neither for the slow of wit nor for the multi-taskers to comprehend.

I had been living at the Plaza for almost a year now. A full-fledged graduated from the rat's intense boot camp, or "Rat-Think U", as we took to calling it. (Mose & Err's course required six months, with periodic refreshers. Our own elite U.S. Marine's 'Boot' only lasts thirteen weeks: the Gyrenes are wimps, compared) When I say 'we' I refer to our little clique of Red & Petal, Julie Andrews and me. No, not *the* Julie Andrews, but a woman who looked just like Julie Andrews did in The Sound of Music. For weeks, I did not know how or why she was recruited - and I did not care, because I was a doting fan of hers the instant I saw her, just like I was with the screen version of Julie Andrews. Her tag read "Julie" and her smell was a mixture of honey and sweat. I guess that translates to a desire for fame; but what's wrong with that?

Julie Andrews and Red were roommates. They lived in an apartment in the Trump Tower a few blocks down from me on Fifth Avenue. I did not yet completely trust Red - as you can imagine. I was scared stiff of her. For some reason she never figured me out. It probably had something to do with my scent. Anyway, Julie Andrews and Red & Petal used to come over to my place after the Rat-think sessions and we'd sit on my terrace overlooking Central Park. We'd gossip about the Chumpers and the various rats we had gotten to know. We'd de-brief. They were good times - except for the tension caused by my unbridled fear of Red.

It was shortly after we had unlearned all the Ten Commandments when Red burst in my apartment with Julie Andrews and shouted, "Did you hear? Bacci is dead!" Red broke down in tears. Petal moped by Red's ankles, not knowing how to help. Julie Andrews quietly wept, it was so sweet a weeping I had a little bitty of a thought she might have been faking it - for show. But she was sincere. My suspicions were born from my lack of a healthy emotional upbringing. No matter, it was a good show and I wanted to hug her, but I was afraid she would pull away. So, I stood there, not knowing how to feel – because I never knew how or what to feel about anything, really. This comes from growing up in a broken home, I guess. But I could make it look like I was feeling something by making my mouth twitch. … And pretending to gasp I blurted out, "Oh, my God? How? When? This is terrible."

It was worse than terrible. Here was the situation as best we knew it at the time: It turns out Bacci was giving one of her BOFFO dinners to a bunch of new Chumpers across town. Typical of me, my first tingling of an emotion was I was upset to hear Bacci was making appearances without me. *'Who was she using as a translator?'* I wondered. Then I felt uneasy and guilty at the same time. I mean Bacci had just passed away and all I could think of was: *'Where do I fit in?'*

Apparently, she had been doing her hovering act when one of the Chumpers at the table - a former Governor of California/ action hero movie actor, jumped on top of the table and did a kick box maneuver to Bacci's underside, which killed her while she was floating in mid-air. The whole thing went down faster than a speeding bullet, as many horrific events do. The terrible deed occurred so fast the rats and the Chumpers could not believe their eyes. While Bacci slowly sunk to the tabletop, like a balloon with a slow leak, the ex-governor movie actor fled the room.

'This murderous act and ensuing escape went so smoothly, it must have been pre-planned,' I thought. "HHHmmm."

Someone wrapped a fold of the tablecloth over Bacci's dead body. Within seconds the rats started to understand what had happened. A hundred thousand rats moaning and groaning and cheeking. It must have been a terrible scene. Imagine being a Chumper in such a room. They were pretty scared, so I am told. The Chumpers formed a tight grouping and edged towards the door. It looked like trouble ahead under the subway station on 73rd and Broadway. But then an amazing thing happened; Bacci's body disappeared.

A small pack of rats had come to the table to take Bacci's body to some rat ceremonial place, or something, who knows with rats - but one moment she was lying dead upon the table, under the table cloth, resting over a bed of decomposing vegetables - and the next: she was gone into thin air. Yes. That is what is told.

And the whole pack of Chumpers and Rats fell on their respective knees in awe. (Do you remember? I *told* you earlier that Awe is a feature in this story.)

Well!

Back in my apartment in the Plaza we did not know what to do. I was confused, filling up with dread and with more than a twinge of foreboding. Was Bacci killed by a permanently insane madman? Was this some stupid, audacious act of an attention needy fool? Or was this a conspiratorial act? Was there more than one person involved? Was there a counter-rat movement afoot? Was this Judas Chumper a tool of a rival rat group? Where was the recently divorced ex-governor movie actor – and why was he in town? Where? What? Were we uncovered? By humans? What? Who benefits now?

When Red ran out of tears, she pulled herself together and put on a face devoid of any emotion. She looked more alert than I had ever seen her. She would be strong no matter what was coming. She was truly the Alpha female. I thought Red would be good to have with you in a foxhole situation. But me, I do not like foxholes. I'd rather be with someone who could help me get out of a foxhole, not dig a better one. And we were digging ourselves into a deep, deep hole. I had become aware the rats, with this dead and disappearing Bacci business, had just got Religion. Got a religion of their own. And you know how Religion can cause problems in this world; especially if the Religion is not yours.

We went down to the Plaza's basement where was gathered every Chumper I had ever seen - along with what must have been a hundred fifty thousand rats.

....

One last time; I will respond to another nit-picking question from my editor, which was: How do I know how many rats there were in the basement?

Well, duh, I do not know, exactly. But I have always been good at guessing the size of the crowd at sporting events and rock concerts. I am usually within a couple thousand when they announce the attendance during the seventh inning stretch - that sort of thing. OK: It does not take much brainpower to calculate a lot of rats, maybe fifteen of them, can stand where one adult human can stand. And one adult can stand on one square foot. And, In this case at the Plaza, with my natural feel for how many people it would take to fill the rat part of the room, which covers probably ten thousand square feet, that translates into ten thousand people you could cram down there if each person stood on a square foot - and then you multiply by fifteen. Presto! You have a hundred-fifty thousand rats. Geez, stop it with the questions.

Back to the story.

....

Nobody in the basement knew what was going on. The place stunk to high heaven with fear, let me tell you. Then Err scurried upon the stage at the far end of the room. His grisly features appeared on huge jumbo-tron screens which some Chumper had mounted on to the four walls of the cavernous room. The little rat had a radio piece in an ear and a mike wrapped around the front of his muzzle. Mose, sitting upon his haunch, was right behind Err. Mose's face looking out from way up above on the screens, over our heads, his eyes staring at a spot a thousand yards off - as if he were seeing something of interest from far away. Four gigantic Mose rat faces dominating the great sub-hall. It was weird. You should have been there to see it. Mose acting as if he were inspired; if a rat can look inspired. I never could figure that guy out, whether or not he was for real; but it did not matter what I thought - the crowd was psyched up to hear whatever Mose & Err were going to say.

Err beckoned me to come to the stage along with Red and Julie Andrews. My function was to simultaneously translate to the Chumpers what Err was saying to the rats. My voice going live feed over the visual. While I was back-stage I had noticed we were on a City-wide audio-video hook-up. It seemed to me Mose & Err had things pretty much organized, pretty much too soon, if one were to ask me; but no one did.

I also found it a bit disconcerting that Err had stopped speaking directly to the Chumpers in English. He would only speak in formal Rat tongue, or back-throat, if you will. He was always using me to translate for him. I knew this was some kind of an act and I did not get it. Maybe it was a sign of his contempt for our ways – not deigning to speak our language, now that we knew he could. Yes, it meant job security for me, and I appreciated that, but at the same time it was off-putting.

Red's job was to watch the crowd - look for deviants, maybe co-conspirators. I did not watch her to see if she deleted anybody from the crowd. Her work made me feel uncomfortable. Somebody had to do it, I guess.

I'll admit, I was nervous, this being my first time going live feed and all.

Then Err spoke for Mose. Imagine. Rats all throughout the City were listening to his raspy and strident voice - and all the Chumpers were hoping to get direction from mine.

Right out of the box Err told the multitude was to keep calm. Err proclaimed nothing was seriously amiss. Yes, it was terrible what happened, but it had to happen, for Bacci had foretold her passing. Foretold it to Mose & Err. So said Err. Bacci would not leave us. She was with us in spirit, said Err. Mose looked out as if in rapture, as Err spoke to the multitude, "Do not worry. Bacci will return before the end of The Age of The Dominance of Humans. It is all going as necessary."

Err spoke to the crowd for about ten minutes. He said Mose would lead them to the future and would keep the promise of Bacci. He said the movement was growing quick and strong, "Cheek" there would be safety and peace and abundance in the near times."

'Movement?...near times?' I thought. *"HHHmmm."*

And then Err looked out as if directly talking to the Chumpers everywhere, "Do as you are told. Believe us; we will take care of you. Good care of you. Cheek. Cheek". A dramatic pause, and then as thunderous as a rat could, "Long live Bacci!"

I heard a hundred fifty thousand rats 'Cheek' and squeak and screech in their rat tongue, "Long live Bacci!"

And then I saw my human companions, over fifty Chumpers, rise to their feet and chant; first with some trepidation, and soon thereafter with loud enthusiasm, "Long live Bacci!"

'Jesus Christ!' I said to myself, to my surprise, for I never swear. Imagine; this was playing out all over town, rats and Chumpers cheeking and yelling "Long live Bacci!" and me leading the cheer. I was a tad proud of myself - and ashamed at the same time.

And then Julie Andrews came to the stage. Until that moment I had not seen her in action and had not understood her function, or value to our group. You see, Julie Andrews could sing. Oh my, could she sing.

● ●

Here is where I have to back up a bit. Catch you up on a body of Rat Knowledge - so you can understand what you are about to see.

Back in the 1950's and 1960's, the Rockefeller Institute (which is located on York Avenue over by the East River), did hundreds of studies (which is a euphemism for 'experiments') on rats. I will talk more of these *studies* later for the discovering of The Lost Rockefeller Files may have prolonged my career and saved my life to this very moment. But for now, it is enough to say many of these experiments dealt with how many sound and decibel variants (noise, harmonious, etc.) animals can tolerate under all sorts of conditions. These studies proved fruitless in they bore no conclusions which could be turned into discovering a new pain-killer drug, or better yet, a lethal weapon.

Remember when our troops blasted music and drove Noriega crazy down in Panama, with Judas Priest's "You've Got Another Thing Coming", followed by Brenda Lee's great, "Crying In The Chapel"? Meatloaf was also on the Noriega Top Ten. Remember that? Well, the submerged music technique was first fathomed by a grad student doing a term paper titled

"Rodent/Noise Study #132: Proving The Ability To Drive Rodents Insane Through The Medium of Various Sounds; Harmonious and Not." -Molly Jones, 1965

Molly's paper received a B+. The rats experimented upon were thrown unceremoniously into the East River. That study and many others which drew provocative conclusions were never looked at by any serious group, for over fifty years, never scrutinized, until I found them and forwarded them to the rat geeks. These papers were and are a virtual treasure trove of salient information pertaining to rat - and as important: human behavior. They served to confirm to those with a negative bias towards humans how cruel we could be in search of a master's degree - let alone in the quest for something which could earn a credit for a term paper. The Rockefeller files have been submitted as proof positive to the rats that Humans were, at best, heartless. Furthermore, the evidence showed: Human beings were not in the best interests regarding the survival of rats. Very important, these documents.

One of the vital facts the rat-geeks uncovered from those works was: Rats love music. Not all music. But what they do love really moves them, uncontrollably. Of course, rats have known for thousands of years that they love music, but only recently did some of them find that they could control other rats with music. Yes. Rats can be controlled by certain pieces of music.

Remember this because it may come in handy to you someday. It might save your life.

End of Chapter 7

"Bert and His Mom"

Everybody was amazed to see how large Bert grew. He is a gentle giant, the way a lot of huge creatures are.

CHAPTER 8

ACID

"The garbage of the rich is no better than the garbage of the poor"
-Excerpted from Mathuzala's columns in https://
notesfromtheroomofwonder.com

. . . .

(We pick up our dictation after a small lunch break)

...Where were we? Oh Yes. Julie Andrews.

The crowd - especially the rat segment of it - was getting unruly. What with the 'cheek, cheeking' and many of them rolling over and meeping and others doing that tight circling thing they do like they are trying to chase their tail. I thought somebody should do something. Soon.

And then Julie Andrews stepped out onto the center stage - and into control of the situation.

She held a hand-mike and behind her were those gigantic amp speakers, stacked high, which you usually see at mega-rock concerts. Down by her feet she had one of those foot pedaled pedals which she could tap on - and out would come back-ground beats and pre-arranged accompaniments. The singing started. Soft and slow. What was it? That piece? It was the most beautiful music I had ever heard. Julie Andrews looked straight into the soul of all of us - she owned the room - and she belted out the Flower Duet, the classic aria from Dussek's Lakme. Incredibly, Julie Andrews sang both parts of the duet. I Googled it to find out what it was. You could Google it too. Then go to: Leo Delves, Dorme Epais - Act 1. Do that now and you will hear what I am talking about. The rats heard. They were transfixed. They could not move in fact. Do you understand what I am saying? The rats remained stock-still while Julie Andrews sang The Flower Duet. I don't know why that is - but there you have it.

Shortly after the crowd had been silenced and stunned into motionlessness, the music sound was turned down and Mose & Err came back on the screens and told everybody not to worry and to fear not about Bacci's cruel and untimely demise. Investigations into the matter were being made. Mose & Err had everything under control. They said, "We are going to meet more often now, and that is a good thing for there is much to do. But for now, let us not weep, let us rejoice in our having known Bacci and take comfort in our closeness - and in our cause."

And then Mose & Err signaled to Julie Andrews to come back for an encore, as if they were running some kind of interspecies Ed Sullivan show. The cameras re-positioned to her while she segued into the best version of "The Stroll" I have ever heard. She could go from a high operatic C to a baritone bass note as easy as you please. Why she never made an appearance on American Idol, I'll...well actually I did find out - I'll tell you later about that sorry tale.

Have you ever seen a hundred and fifty thousand rats doing "The Stroll"? I don't think so, unless you are a Chumper. It is a wondrous sight. You should'a been there. Somehow the rats knew how to line dance - as good as people; but with fewer inhibitions. For the moment, the rats had forgotten their agony over losing their marvelous and amazing leader. They were totally occupied getting the dance just right. And they did. We Chumpers were all clapping and having a good time.

And then Julie Andrews picked up the pace with a show stopping rendition of D.J. Casper's "Cha-Cha Electric Slide". (U-tube this number and you will get it.)

The house went crazy. Every, rat out on the floor hopping about, putting one foot forward and then the next, "Move to the left. Now move to the right. Take it back, y'all!

Slide to the left. Now to the right.... One hop this time." Julie Andrews belting out the orders and more rats than you have ever seen - in lock step and hopping about and turning around on command. "Clap your hands, y'all!" And the rats all beat their gnarly fore claws together. It looked like great fun.

"Take it back, y'all! ...Two hops this time. ..." and the Chumpers were now on the floor and the place was really jumping. "Now give it the Cha-Cha slide!"

And then an odd thing - I looked off to stage right and I noticed Mose & Err were not dancing. They were watching the display on the floor like proud parents would watch their children. At least that is how it appeared to me. Err was poking Mose with one of those disgusting non-opposing thumbs of his, as if to say "See, I told you so." Or "Look. This is good!" Then Mose said something back to him, I could not tell what it was because I can't read rat-lips. But *Mose* was talking. He was not a mute, after-all. *"HHHmmm"*, I thought.

"Three hops this time...Now turn around...clap your hands, y'all!" Everybody gave it their best. Even Red. She was a terrific dancer; wild but controlled. The music was a good thing, for sure. Another thing I noticed was even though Red was dancing - and she was as good at it as any rat or Chumper out there - she was constantly checking the room looking to see who was not participating. I danced. You better believe.

Err gave a sign to Julie Andrews and she ended it with the Cha-Cha number to give the crowd a bit of a rest. But you could tell everybody wanted more. A few seconds later Julie Andrews glanced at Err and he nodded back, and Julie started on a number that was a bastardization of one of Tupac Shakur's obscene rant raps. (Do not bother to Google or Pandora this.)

Suddenly the rats started to twitch and look about. Then they appeared agitated, no, make that: They were greatly disturbed. Julie Andrews sang words which she interspersed with rat noises, cheeks and meeps and rat words that were shocking in their bad taste. Words used in a way which rats hitherto had never thought of, even in their darkest moments. Human creations of foul word/thoughts translated into rat-speak. Rats, in their thousands of years of feasting on this planet, had never realized such dreck could be imagined or uttered aloud. Words conveying the meaning of body activity, body parts and body waste - as if something were wrong with these. The deduction to make is: Rats cannot abide the very intent of and use of foul language - I am not talking swear words - but foul, dirty words like: 'piss' and 'turd' and 'ass'. Rats cannot stand those types of words, whether they be in human or rat tongue.

I remember reading a study to this effect which I had recovered from deep in the Rockefeller Files. A certain Jason Jarrett, working for a Doctorate in 1963, had done a paper on experiments which had subjected rats to a constant bombardment of filthy talk and disgusting sounds. In his seminal work, he noticed that rats were quick to respond to these noises and always did so, violently. Unfortunately, Mr. Jarrett's paper was ridiculed. In point of fact he was asked to take a leave of absence from the Institute and was not awarded his Doctorate there. The Rockefeller staff incorrectly thought Mr. Jarrett was addicted to obscene sounds and was, therefor, not up to their lofty standards. This was a mistake, for there was much to be learned from his particular Rat/ Noise studies.

So. The rats I was looking at in the Plaza's basement obviously hated the very essence of the words of Tupac's rap rant. Out there, on the floor, it was a madding and throbbing mosh-pit like you have never seen. In the rats' agitation, they were scratching and turfing as if to advance in a menacing manner towards... towards the Chumpers. One hundred fifty thousand disturbed, riled up rats who looked like they had harmful, toxic, acid in their drool - moving forward, towards us Chumpers to what end; I could only tremble at the thought. Imagine this going on in live streaming, screaming screens in basements all over the City. It was awful. The terror seemed to last forever; but it was only for about five seconds or so.

Err moved next to Julie Andrews, who quick cut back to "The Flower Duet" - thank you very much - and the rooms across the City fell silent. The cameras focused on Mose one more time who looked out on us in a paternal manner, if a rat can look paternal - and Err said, "Thank you, everybody. That is all for tonight. We will get together again soon; in a few days. ...Before the Operations begin."

End of Chapter 8

Oh, before we end with this Chapter, let me give you some advice: If you possibly can: Learn to sing the Flower duet. Just in case. It will stop the rats cold. This is a difficult number to master, too difficult for the average singer. So, failing that, learn to sing/lead the Cha-Cha Electric Slide and practice a Von Trapp family type of escape and get the heck out of wherever you are when the time comes. Do not depend upon a boom box or anything with wires to play these songs for you - because the rats will nibble through the cables and what have you. Playing little iddy-bitty iPods and cellphones won't do the trick either. The rats do not buy it. The sound on these devices is too tinny. As far as I can tell you can only count on live performances to affect the rats. I do not know why this is. Of course, Julie Andrews could control them over live video – but she was exceptional – and she had big equipment. Remember what I tell you. Start practicing.

The real end to Chapter 8

"Pammy"

Pammy is off to the side, like a little wallflower - watching Red & Petal as they do the Cha-Cha Electric Slide. She hopes, she can join in on the fun, someday. Pammy is a timid little thing.

CHAPTER 9

HOMELESS

"Work is failure. Your species cannot grasp this morsel of truth - and that failing is contributing significantly to the Downfall of the Humans." -Excerpted from Mathuzala's columns in: https://notesfromtheroomofwonder.com

•••

You know how troubles always come in threes?

The night I just told you about with the hullabaloo in the basement of The Plaza was Trouble Number One. Trouble Number Two relates to my mom, who at that same time was lying in comfort in a comatose state in hospice. Trouble Number Three - well, we'll get there after I finish telling you more about Trouble Number Two.

Do you remember my telling you I donated an entire floor to the Mount Sinai Hospital with my newfound riches? It is true. Floor Nineteen is a high-toned geriatric ward for those in need of hospice. It may be the best run and most expensive unit of its kind in the country.

I have wanted to do something for my mom ever since I was a kid. Ever since I learned she became clinically depressed after giving birth to me. She often told me that immediately after my delivery; she fell into a dark pit of despair. Deeper and deeper she went as each day passed. Post-Partum Depression they called it - and I was the Partum. Can you imagine the guilt put upon me at the most tender of age?

Well! She lapsed into a catatonic state a few years ago. It was Plato, actually, who had suggested I fund and create the floor for her, in her honor - and to take care of her, of course. The rats contributed, financially, to the cause with a fervor you would not believe. They brought all kinds of fabulous baubles to my apartment. Some I have not been able to dispose of to this day - for I fear art treasure detectives are looking for several pieces of the loot. I thank the rats for what they did. I never saw any verifiable improvement in mom's condition at the ward; but she was comfortable there, for a long time. At least that is something.

So, …

The night after Julie Andrew's Big Dance I went straight to Mom's room, to get away from it all - and try to make sense of what was going on. As I told you before, I went to her room almost every evening.

But on this particular evening Mom was gone.

"She up and left," the nurses said. Mom, they said, suddenly burst out of her coma and was spitting mad. She said she wanted, "…to get the Goddamned Hell out of this rat-hole," to quote her. Mom was a swearer, so I knew they were talking about the right woman. The staff had been of the opinion they had no legal right to hold her against her will. They also had no idea where she was going. *'Geez oh, Pete',* I thought. That was Trouble Number Two.

Number Three was: There was a strange, old man in her bed. The Geriatric/Hospice Floor was always full up with a waiting line out the door and around the block. Therefore, I assumed management, not wishing to have a useless vacancy - and wasting no time - gave mom's bed to the next person who came off the streets. This particular one looked horrible. He was A filthy, sickly, homeless man. Wheezing and coughing. He had bad breath - probably halitosis; but I'm not a doctor.

In an attempt at gathering my wits, I sat down in the chair right next to the homeless man, where I would have sat if my mom had been there. "Get me a private eye, or Pinkerton or somebody. Bring her back here!" I barked to the nurses, thinking if they found her, they'd have to up her meds asap. "…Put out a search party – now!" I mean I was the guy who paid for everything here. I had the right to boss people around - when push came to shove. No?

The nurses scurried out of the room.

I got up and locked the door good and tight. Then I went into

Mathuzala's chamber, which is behind the trap door in the closet off the rear wall in mom's private bathroom.

Who is Mathuzala? Mathuzala is my favorite rat, ever. I first came across Mathuzala around the same time we put mom in her bed - about six months prior to her sudden departure. He was very old when I met him. Remember, the average rat lives about eighteen months - but Mathuzala was already over four years old when he moved into our new facility. The rats had built him the best hospital room I have ever seen. It has every piece of life sustaining equipment imaginable. State of the art.

Mathuzala, you see, had been the victim of rat experiments - conducted on the now infamous Plum Island. In his case, the crazed scientists wanted to see what they could do to prolong life; slow down the aging process. They fed him a strict diet of high protein green vegetables. They also opened his brain and into the area behind his cerebral cortex, and just over his amygdala - the place where the mind is supposed to be found – and then they infused it with a shot of a mixture of a performance enhanced steroid and adrenalin. The result was his brain, especially the mind part of it, grew and functioned at a higher level of any brain than ever recorded in history. He can ingest big data and connect all the dots. He can prophesy – when he wants. And why doesn't anybody know this? Because exactly at the time Mathuzala's mind was gigantic sizing, a TV network crew came to Plum Island and exposed on national broadcast the inhumane treatment the 'scientific' fiends were perpetrating on the lab rats.

Shortly after the exposing of the grisly Plum Island experiments to the world, the 'Research Center' was de-funded and the animals were let loose. 'Discarded' would be a better term. Fortunately, Mathuzala's fellow rats found him floating amongst the flotsam and jetsam down by the Battery docks, before the currents took him out to the Atlantic – where he would have been lost forever. The rats gave him succor and brought him to my Nineteenth Floor. Perhaps I have it backwards. Perhaps, the rats found me, and gave me riches and had me build the geriatric ward with the secret room - just so they could save and savor Mathuzala. Either way, it is good enough for me, because Mathuzala has made my life worth living.

So, as I was saying, I entered his room.

"I know what happened at the Plaza. And I have heard about your mom, my Little Pea-pod." Mathuzala called me his 'Little Pea-pod'. He had grown to love me, I could tell. A shrink might say he was to me a replacement for a father image, a father I never had – but he was more than that.

Mathuzala was a Human Whisperer, my own personal whisperer, and I trusted him with my every fiber. He had the adorable habit of filling his mouth up with air, puffing up his cheeks to the point they would look like they were going to pop and then he would push the air out - and then he would speak. Puff. Blow. It was really cute; I wish you could have seen him. Except, because of his being all hooked up on all the hospital devices he would not have wanted you to see him that way.

He could not say "Cheek" like the others. It must have been a cleft pallet problem, no doubt a carry-over from some horrible experiment on Plum Island. Either way "Cheek" sounded more like; "*Chleezk*". It was a nice sound, actually.

Puff. Blow. Smoke would come out of his mouth and nostrils as he exhaled, because he had been addicted to tobacco during several experiments on Plum Island. He must have smoke four packs a day. He also has a terrible cough.

(You might notice I speak of Mathuzala in both the past and present tense. This is because though Mathuzala is no longer with us, in this dimension – he is still here, with us in another. Much will be explained as we go further into our story.)

"Don't worry about your Mom. We will find her." Puff. Blow. ..."Chleezk." "Cough, cough." He had the most soothing voice I ever heard. It sounded just like Morgan Freeman speaking. Imagine Morgan Freeman calling you his "Little Pea-pod". It does not get much better than that. Then Mathuzala took a sip of juice from the plastic straw which had been vel-cro'd near his mouth, which was attached to a tube hanging down from a liquid feeder bag, adjacent to the plasma pouch which was constantly circulating fluids through his tiny body. "We have a bigger problem right now than your mom running about through the city." Sip. "The bad news is: Mose & Err have gone rogue. It was they who orchestrated the killing of Bacci. There will be no trial. No justice. The ex-governor was in on the charade. *Chleezk*." "Cough, cough."

"But how?" I asked, dumbfounded.

"*How* is not important, Little Pea-pod. But *Why*? *Why* is the problem.

And what we need to do about it is of ultimate concern, for you and I at the moment are the only hope there is to stop Mose & Err in their tracks. Unfortunately, you are merely a Chumper; having little suasion with your kind and you will soon have less, because they will find you out, my little Pea-pod. ... And I am an aging rat, hooked on pain killers with a brain that is about to metastasize and explode, *Chleezk*, perhaps within the next thirty days." "Cough, cough."

"Oh no, Mathuzala, you cannot die!" I was so emotionally wrenched I had not focused on his mention of my being found out. That would be Trouble Number Four.

Just to let you know how bad my evening went - when I left Mathuzala's room that night, after four hours of talking and strategizing about matters of 'ultimate concern' for the rats, the human race and the planet in general - I stepped back into mom's room and the homeless man in her bed signaled for me to come near him so I could hear what he had to say. And when I bowed down to his smelly mouth, he rasped, menacingly, into my ear, "We know what you are doing."

End of Chapter 9

"Frank"

To an unpracticed eye, one would think this is a picture of Pammy. One would be wrong. Frank is male. His ears are different, among other things. No two rats are exactly alike – just like no two humans are exactly alike.

CHAPTER 10

COMMENTARY

"So, you are in a maze - and you know where the cheese is. Do you always go directly for the cheese? Or do you roam the maze for the heck of it, for the wonder of it all? ...Simply to see what is what? ...Tell me, my little Pea-pod. Chleezk. Puff. Blow." "Cough, cough." -Excerpted from https://notesfromtheroomofwonder.com

• •

Words cannot adequately express the stress this added to my night. My temples throbbed. If you had been there you would have seen the little blue vein thing of mine which bulges out of my forehead when I feel threatened. It is a primitive, natural physical response, I suppose. The old man continued to talk; but I could barely hear what he was saying because of the blood rushing around noisily in my head. I took deep breaths and started to count - slowly - to ten. And then a quiet peace came over me and I knew there was no problem that Mathuzala and I could not handle - if I stayed calm.

So. Let me tell you a little bit more of my experiences with Mathuzala – and you will understand how I came to trust myself and how I handled the situation with the intrusive old man:

Coincidentally, earlier that very night, while sitting at Mathuzala's feet, or hind claws, he addressed me thusly:

"It has been said, my Little Pea-pod: 'When the problem is identified, it is half solved.' Wrong. Studies prove most of the world's problems are the result of solutions to previous problems. Hence, when the problem has been identified, the number of problems actually progress geometrically. The formula is: ½ x's the number (#) of those acquainted with the situation of concern, multiplied by the speed of darkness divided by the weight of the applied gravity. Chleezk. Puff. Blow." Sip. "Wheeze." Mathuzala was a genius. This is how he started off that night, the long night when we discussed the situation of Mose & Err and the killing of Bacci and the Big Dance.

For more than six months, I had sat at Mathuzala's bedside, comforting him and holding his tiny little claw-paws in my hands, I had become adept at translating his thoughts, which might have seemed obtuse to the poorly informed - which is most everybody. What I am saying is I became Mathuzala's interpreter and amanuensis. Like the guy who wrote what the Prophet had to say, like the guys who wrote what the Teacher said - that is *me,* for Mathuzala - and I do not care who knows it. But remember, I am only the messenger. The commentary is not mine.

So.

Decoding the above hypothesis: Mathuzala was talking about Mose & Err and the advent of their schism. A radical and soon to be violent rat movement. A new problemo. No sooner had Bacci and her pack assembled a team, replete with Chumper Chapters, for the purpose of altering the impact the Human Race was having on Earth - than did Mose & Err come up with another approach on how to handle the situation. A whole new brace of difficulties ensued.

Mathuzala had intuited that Mose & Err feared Bacci's approach was too conciliatory, too obscure, and too non-direct. Mose & Err had lost patience with Bacci. They thought it was going to take too much time for the Chumpers to gain enough power to change the harmful patterns set and entrenched by the Human institutions. On top of that, they thought Bacci was 'losing it' and spinning (or hovering) out of control. She was giving the game plan away. For example, she had recently told a fledgling Chumpers group in SOHO about how the rats were going to eat through all the fiber-optic wires, the cables of cars, the wiring of aircraft, of everything...all this with a lot of "Cheeks" from mid-air. Yes. Bacci had bragged on and on and divulged much of the Rat Plan for Deconstruction and Disruption.

(An aside here: Much like the Wizard in the Wizard of Oz, Mathuzala, behind the curtain, suggested the 'In Obscuritas, Securitas Est' motif for the Chumpers' dinners. He believed a covert, anonymous, obscure program was ideal and necessary to successfully begin a revolutionary movement. Mathuzala was *the thinker* and prime mover. It was Mathuzala who re-wrote the Commandments for the humans. Mose & Err entered the scene as teachers - as facilitators; but now they had become something else.

Mose & Err took it into their own claws and thumbs to start anew. And the killing of Bacci as a solution created a veritable hornets' nest, which is an apt metaphor, for hornets were not good news to rats. Mathuzala, far from the fronts, resting in hospice with wonder drugs flowing through his veins, figured out that there was a new game in town and hostilities were about to begin. Sooner than later. The speed of darkness was picking up, yet the weight of applied gravity, the denominator, had the integrity of something between one and zero. That was what Mathuzala was concerned with.

The upstart teachers had considered Bacci to be dangerous to the cause with her arrogance and her floating act. They saw her as morally weak, wallowing in her human admirers and, ... and Mose & Err felt they were better fit to handle things from then on. Don't you be surprised. Same thing happens with human movements, you know that – if you read newspapers, or the incoming alerts on your phone.

So. They arranged her martyrdom, thinking: No Bacci equals no problem. The movement gets a saint out of the deal. And Mose & Err are in position to take over the whole shebang. Enough of these boot-camps; they are a waste of time. School was over. The rats wanted to go with the troops they had. The day Bacci was exterminated, was the new 'Day One' - according to Mose & Err. B.C. and C.E are over. It is now A.B. 'After Bacci'. And Mose & Err are in charge, leading living creatures to the New Era: The time of Mose & Err.

Unless, of course, Mathuzala and I could do something about it.

The problem is: The rats have already started to nibble. Have you checked your computer lately? Better back up everything on your computers: Twice. Watch out for flash trade errors on the Stock Exchanges. Watch for power plants shutting down. You'll see electricity going down all over the world.

It is not in big scale just yet. They started testing on week One, A.B. Testing for real. It seemed nobody out there had figured it out. Maybe that guy in mom's bed knew something. I'll get back to him in a minute.

A little bit more about Mathuzala first; because he is such a national treasure – and knowing more of him may explain a lot to you.

He had a mild form of Gillet de la Tourette's Syndrome. A lot of genius's have it. The Trainman, John Nash - the mathematician. Me - I have it too. I do not swear uncontrollably, like some do with the affliction. In my case, I am abnormally gifted with numbers and computer engineering. Symptoms vary.

Mathuzala told me *they* accidentally gave it to him on Plum Island. As I told you before, the craven scientists hoped to learn something about the subject of longevity; but the experiment backfired and Mathuzala learned more about them than the other way around. What happened was Mathuzala's brain grew at an alarming rate and the scientists realized he was becoming smarter than anybody ever recorded. They were about to pull the plug on him, literally, but it was exactly at this time Plum Island was defunded. The scientists did not know that, somehow, Mathuzala's mind was so advanced it was communicating directly to the Cloud. All the information that was shooting up into the cloud and floating around there, over five trillions of new bits every second, was Mathuzala's playground. And during the long periods of the day when I was not visiting with him, he was stomping around in the cloud. He was unto himself a virtual browser, bigger than Google, Yahoo and that Chinese site all put together. (Unfortunately, for me, Mathuzala was spending more and more time up there and I knew someday he would not come back.)

A side effect of his constantly being overloaded with facts and bytes was he was constantly chattering and uncontrollably burbling about what he was learning up there. If you did not pay close attention to what he was saying, you might think he was some mad, ranting fool of a rat. However, if you focused on his words - well, they were not loony-bin ravings, but learned pathways to wisdom and more.

Another thing the mad scientists did not know was: Shortly after Mathuzala was rescued from Plum Island, he mated with dozens of rats. Yes. Mathuzala has thousands of children and tens of thousands of grandchildren. I have met some of them. They look just like the old man, make that old rat. What with their enlarged pre-frontal cortex's they had enhanced reasoning abilities and were much cuddlier in appearance than their ancestors. '*HHHmmm*', you should be thinking. They are disarming, these smarties. We'll get back to them later.

A few months ago, after I realized the wonder and value of Mathuzala's utterances I took it upon myself to record his words by placing a little tape recorder next to his chin whiskers. Each morning - after visiting him, I transcribed his ruminations and backed them up twice - and, yes, I sent them back to the cloud. In fact, I have even heard Mathuzala refer to some of his own facts and quotes which he, himself, had deposited in the cloud several weeks previously. If you are interested, in reviewing some of the knowledge of which I speak, you may go to https://notesfromtheroomofwonder.com

And you will come to know what I know.

End of Chapter 10

"Ginger & Fred"

"Do you want to jump on one of those Cruise ships? Ginger asks Fred. "They have heaps of food and lots of music we can dance to." "I'm dressing up my tail." Says Fred. Ginger knows a thing or two about boats. Her ancestors came over on the Mayflower.

CHAPTER 11

Thrill

"Hear now the great unwanted truth: Humans cannot afford civilization. They cannot even afford to put out their fires. This is not a metaphor. That is a fact. And *that* is a problem. Chleezk." Sip. Puff. Blow. -Excerpted from: https://notesfromtheroomofwonder.com

- -

So. Where was I? Oh, yes. "We know what you are up to," said the man who was supposed to be convalescing in Mom's bed. Mom, gone to who knows where. Mathuzala informing me he is going to die. Mathuzala telling me I had to skulk around and find out who in my Chumpers' group I can trust. The Congressmen? The lobbyists? The CEO's? The former President of the United States? (I think not.) And only recently I learned you can't even trust the former Governor of California - and he having been an action hero. Who can you trust? Geez.

Would Red have me off'd if she scented *I* was on the wrong side of Mose & Err? Now there were several sides and it was becoming difficult to settle on which was what and where you should be. It was like an ever-shifting Rubik's cube and all the colors were staying scrambled no matter which I twisted and turned. At this time, I took to frequently rubbing my temples to keep the throbbing down. It worked while I rubbed, and I got a little relief while I tried to think.

If those rats Mose & Err suspected me of not going with the new movement, or whatever it was; was I a goner? ...After all the good work I had done for the cause? What if they found out Mathuzala was setting up a clandestine meeting for me with some of his kin, his tribe as it were. What had I gotten into?

...And now this creepy old man in mom's bed. I responded to him as pleasantly as possible.

"Pardon me? What? What did you say?" I asked, trying to be casual. *Who was he? What was his game?*

The old buzzard wheezed, "I said 'We know what you are doing'. And we are watching you." He rasped as if he were awfully sick and unhealthy. If he was acting, he was very good at it. His rheumy eyes rolled around in their sockets, not focusing on anything. The rantings of a dying man? I think not.

His mouth was dry, and his voice crackled, "You go into that bathroom. You lock yourself in and transmit classified information, or Anti-American schemes to the enemy. We hear your voice in the bathroom - and we hear coded noises coming back to you. We don't know where you get the information from. Or what you are sending. Yet! We don't even know who you are sending it to. Probably the Russians or some Al Qaeda group, maybe the Taliban...but we know you are up to something...and we are on to you."

Humans do strange things when they are full of fear. And I am human. Maybe that explains why without thinking, or premeditation, really, I decided not to continue offering my charity to this particular patient. You could say I became a 'death panel' of one, in that I figuratively pulled the plug on this old man's ersatz support systems. I gently pushed a few buttons, which gave the appearance on the monitors that some attendant had, inadvertently, over-medicated him. And the medications flowed accordingly. It was a no-no, I'll admit it. But it had been a long night and I was not at my best. I tell myself that I exercised my right to defend myself. Fight or flight, I say. I chose to fight. I can live with that. Anyway, this old geezer occasionally comes back to haunt me. So, he gets even.

Thinking back on it, I wish I had not done what I did, exactly then. I would have benefitted from knowing who this man was, who sent him. Who were *they* who sent him to Mom's chambers in the first place? Was he from The Agency? The Feds? What? From another group of rats? I knew Mathuzala would figure it all out. Nevertheless, psychologically,

I was somewhere between high anxiety and panic – and cannot be held responsible for my actions at that time. I thought my agita was going to do me in.

The big question I had, the one that came from my burning gut was: "Was I safe?" Going back into Mathuzala's room right now was not a good idea, what with a dead man in Mom's bed and doctors, nurses and admin types soon to crowd the scene.

After helping the staff with the tedious paperwork details caused by a deceased patient in the ward, I repaired to the Plaza.

I remember thinking how lovely Central Park looks in the spring, with balloons and kites stuck in trees and all the good- looking people in their jogging outfits and the little children walking with their little doggies, or parents, or nannies, or whoever they were walking with. It was bizarre. Here I was a recent killer, (albeit with a 'Stand your ground' kind of self-defense - you have to admit,) motherless, and possibly a target for some power mad rats - and all I could think of was how nice the Plaza looked in that morning light; like some huge post renaissance American Beauty hugging the sky - and me wondering what all these contented people passing me by would think if they knew there were two hundred thousand rats underground just moiling and agitating to put a stop to all our fun.

With these idle thoughts floating through my troubled mind, I massaged my temples good and hard and entered the lobby by the Palm Court side.

Now get this: From out of the blue, there she was. The woman of ...of ... *from* beyond my dreams. On this most horrible of days, the woman I never even dared dream could exist, existed right in front of my eyes. If you don't believe in dumb luck or thunderbolts, you are wrong. I was struck dumb.

Remember I told you about the picture of Eloise which hangs on the wall in the Plaza's hallway leading to the Palm Court? Remember? Well I told you. (Go back and look; you'll see it in the early pages of Chapter 2.)

There she was. Eloise. Standing right in front of me.

She was wearing the same white shirt and black jumper skirt with the black suspender straps that she wore in the painting. And the knee-high white stockings. And the black patent leather flats. She had put on a little weight. What do you expect after more than fifty years?

But gosh almighty, she looked great.

"Do you want a lick of my ice cream?" she asked while holding her double scoop straight out to me.

"Sure I do." I said and took a lick. The thrill of it all. High times.

Me. Lost. On the run, maybe. A target, maybe. Falling in love. Just like in the movies. My publisher approves of this part, you better believe. And the best part is: It is all true.

We went into the Palm court where we had two Vanilla Parfaits and two cups of nice hot tea with milk. We talked for the longest time; but time flew by. If you have ever been in love, you know what I mean.

Eloise had just moved back into the Plaza, having recently purchased one of the larger apartments. Skipperdee, her pet turtle had died years ago, so she was carrying an FAO Schwartz stuffed turtle in his honor. Her doggie, Weenie, was long gone, poor thing. She had never married. The men she had met in life were all drips. She said she did not think I was a drip. I could have died that morning and it would have been a good life - but in truth I wanted more. I knew I wanted to live with Eloise and be her non-drip of a man. *"HHHmmmmmmm"* I emoted.

For a few precious moments I forgot all about Mom, the dead man in her bed, the rats and the humans. It was Eloise, ice cream, hot tea and me. It was all good - for that little twinkle of a crack in time.

End of Chapter 11

"CLYDE & BONNIE"

Bonnie says,"You go look for jewelry and loose cash in Hotel room number 206. I'll go to room 207. We'll deposit whatever loot we have on Benedict's door." "Ok." Says Clyde.

CHAPTER 12

LOVELY

"Hope is false. But it is hope which keeps you going, until there is no hope at all."

-Excerpted from https://notesfromtheroomofwonder.com

••

It had been many months since I had socialized with anyone outside of my rat coterie. I was way out of my comfort zone trying to navigate the social scene. I mean, I could not ask Eloise up to my apartment to check out the view of Central Park, could I? Red and Julie Andrews might be up there. Red snarling all the time, looking for betrayers. And Julie Andrews constantly humming the 'Flower Duet'. What would Eloise think of my friends? Or they of her? Also, there was the likelihood of hundreds of rats running around in my living room - as they had taken a tendency to do lately. Everybody had been taking liberties; but before Eloise came upon the scene I never had any need of privacy.

I was multi-tasking in that I was paying as much attention to Eloise as I could while I was trying to figure out my next move with her, while I was rubbing my temples, while I was trying to be suave at the same time.

When all of a sudden, she asked in her delightfully, silly high-pitched, but cute as a button voice, "Would you like to see my apartment?" Heart be still. Everybody is for somebody – and this Eloise is for me. I of course I wanted to see her apartment more than anything; but I could not go up there just then - what with all my crisis's going on concurrently.

I stammered out that I totally wanted to see her place, but I had a lot to do and maybe we could meet tomorrow. She squeaked, "Oh, goody!" and then she put on a pouty face and in almost a whisper, "Tomorrow is better anyway, because I have a little itty-bitty bit of a rodent problem that I should deal with before I have anybody up."

I must have looked horrified because she quickly blurted to explain, "No. No. Don't be alarmed. The apartment isn't dirty or anything like that. It is...it is…" She seemed at a loss for words. She spoke so quietly and that tiny high pitched voice of hers, I had to hunch up close to her mouth to hear, "It's that when I moved back into the Plaza yesterday...well, there were a bunch of, I guess you would say...a pack of rats in the living room. I know you will think this odd of me...but they seem very nice. They tell me they have been in the Plaza for ever so long, since before Mister Trump's upgrade, even. They knew of me from years ago. And they welcomed me back. ...I do not know what to do with them - I had no idea I could talk to rats...." She looked dazed and confused. Poor thing.

But she could talk to the rats? Could she possibly become one of us - the lucky ones?

I stared at her not knowing what to say. *Comfort her*, I thought.

"I know. I understand. I have rats too. It is not so bad."

Astonishment. Waves of relief flooded over her. For an instant she looked exactly like the little child depicted in the portrait hanging on the wall in the outer hall. And then she shape-shifted into her present form. A couple of feet taller than she was in her earlier days. Maybe a hundred, hundred fifty pounds of fun and life experience added to her frame. She was lovely. We had crossed our first hurdle. We agreed to meet in the Palm Court the next day.

As I approached my apartment, I could hear Julie Andrews belting out a tune from my living room. Anybody who knows anything about music would recognize the song from hearing only three notes from a hundred yards down the hallway. It was "Sittin' In A La La. (Waitin' For My Ya Ya)", the One Hit Wonder, by Joey Dee in 1963 - but vastly improved upon by our Julie Andrews. I opened the door to find her and a hundred dancing rats having a grand old time.

"Geez, would you keep it down. What will the neighbors think?" I was on a high from meeting Eloise, yes, but I was also on a low with my other problems - sort of like having a bi-polar experience with both the poles activated at the same time. I did not mean to be short with Julie Andrews and the rats - but there you have it. Julie Andrews stopped it with the A La La and Ya Ya and she quickly hummed a few bars of the Dorme Epais - and the rats, every one of them stopped, frozen in their tracks - waiting for her next tune, or command.

"Where's Red?" I asked.

"She was called on an emergency of some sort by Mose & Errrrr. I don't know what it is about. She'll be back in a bittt." (Maybe I forgot to tell you, Julie Andrews had this odd speech impediment – almost like a stutter – but more pronounced. It only came up when she spoke. When she sang, words came out letter perfect. I had heard this happens to some Country Western singers; but Julie Andrews case was severe. Lady Luck plays it down the middle sometimes.)

Then, unasked for, Julie Andrews gave me a précis of her recent work. "I've been practicing new numbers for my repertoire. I have twelve songs they can't help but respond tooo." She pointed to the petrified rats. "I can make them pounce, stalk and lunge. The three basic attack moves of mammalszzz. Meatloaf drives them wild. They love 'Bat Out of Helllll'. They do not recognize Justin Bieber as music at all - which I agree with... The classic 'I'll Take Manhattan' totally charges them up-pp. What is really interesting is they hate Johnnie Cashshsh. No. More than that, they are afraid of Johnnie Cash. If you simply say 'Hello, my name is Johnnie Cashshsh,' they will run away in panic-k-k."

'*HHHmmm*', I thought.

She went on and on. When Julie Andrews wasn't singing she had a tendency to talk non-stop, despite her speaking impediment. Except for when Red was around. When Red was around, Julie Andrews seemed at rest and at peace. I don't know why that is; but I never was good at understanding human beings or their relationships.

I told you earlier I'd tell you why Julie Andrews never made it big in American Idol - make that: she never even made it past a try-out. She certainly had the talent to go all the way. So, here it is:

Sadly, Julie Andrews never knew her mom because when Julie Andrews was a baby, her mom ran off with a Wall Street stockbroker, and you know how scummy those guys can be. When Julie Andrews realized her mother was never going to return home again, she developed a speech disorder– which no speech therapist could cure. Julie Andrews grew up watching her dad living somewhere between personal despair and the outward hope that his daughter would become a huge success. The hope part comes from the fact that it turned out Julie Andrews was a musical child prodigy. Something must have moved from her speech capabilities into her singing aptitudes. Who knows about these things? Not me. All she did was sing. All day. All night. And she was good. Julie Andrews' dad sacrificed everything he had for her and paid without reservation for private music lessons. While still a pre-teen, she tried out for the Idol prelims in Cincinnati and was a sure bet to win it all. But her private music teacher and coach, who had misguided dreams about her, ever since he first laid eyes on her ...well, she turned him down flat ...and being both a frustrated pervert and a bad loser, he managed to rig the vote at the local level in favor of the kid who should have been an also ran. This pre-maturated boy was a good looking, ordinary talent who strummed a guitar like he was a Kingston Trio wannabe. He flamed out at the National level. Julie Andrews would have taken it all. Her father went numb in disbelief at the unfairness of it all and tried to shoot the coach - you must have read about it in the papers. He took to drink after he was released from the psyche ward and wasted away in grief. Well, you catch the drift for the rest of the story - except for the surprising part where the rats found Julie Andrews, because they knew she had a gift - and Julie Andrews needed to use her gift. Bacci, in person, or however you say it, made the first approach to Julie Andrews - quite an honor.

Julie Andrews is a nice person on the whole – but there are complications. For example, she told me, late one night, that her fantasy was she would appear at a concert at Yankee stadium where a gaggle of American Idol winners were performing ...and she would belt out a Tupac Shakur number, trashing the whole show with a half a million rats. Julie Andrews had no idea Mose & Err had a bigger, better, more BOFFO act in mind for her. She was on schedule to sing to packed houses of her own.

So, where was I? Oh, yes. I was thinking I wanted to be alone for a while and was about to ask Julie Andrews if she did not mind taking her act and the retinue of rats with her - when there came a loud knocking at my door. It was not a gentle rapping as if someone tapping, tapping at my door. Oh, no! It was a banging, as if someone haranguing at my apartment door.

Christopher E. Metzger

"Let me in, I know you're in there you little,"…and then the voice said a dirty word. It was Mom. How she found me, I'll never know. The *how* was not important. The *what* to do was the prime concern. I pressed my temples real hard. Relief. Then out of nowhere, I had an idea.

I asked Julie Andrews to do me a favor.

End of Chapter 12

"THE CLEAN-UP CREW"

These guys work Yankee Stadium. It's the bottom of the ninth and they are watching the scoreboard. When the humans leave, the Crew can begin their Scavenger Hunt. Game on!

CHAPTER 13

MELANGE

There are over 7 trillion bits of data going to the Cloud every second. Most of the bits are either spam, or are in error, and will remain forever unread, or at the least – never accessed by anybody – or anything. My calculations are not yet finished, but there is a suggestion that over 50% of all internet connections relate to pornography – and all this is up there moiling around. The old axiom of 'Garbage In, Garbage Out' – is no longer is applicable. My observation is: The garbage is staying in and festering, breeding even, up there in the Cloud - and has amassed greater volumes than were existing before it all came in. Re-action has become greater than action. The rules of physics which you have been taught in your schools no longer apply. There will be consequences and the resultant 'Changes' will be extraordinary and unexplainable to those educated in the old ways."

-Excerpted from https://notesfromtheroomofwonder.com

••

Before I go on with the story, I have to talk about something which is bothering me. A little while ago, I overheard my editor having a conversation with my agent. She said, "Do you think Benedict is deranged?" Or "... is going insane?" Something like that. I'm so mad I feel like taking my whole exposé to Simon & Schuster. Let me clear the air for once and for all - and I shout it out: *I AM NOT INSANE.* Insane people do the same thing over and over again and hope for different results. I know *that* much. I do not do the same thing over and over again. Oh, all right, occasionally I do repeat some experiments, but when I do - I get different results, so there.

And another thing: Don't go all clever and think I am speaking in metaphor here. My tale is not about a symbolic reference to the moral and structural decay of the human race - This is about real, honest to gosh RATS and their assault on *US*. Jeeze.

Where was I? ...Oh,

I did not get to hear what my agent said in response to my editor's insulting question regarding my level of sanity; but if she is adding fuel to this preposterous innuendo – I will ask Red to give her a little 'what for'. Me, insane? I think not.

Back to the story:

Let me talk about the way I handled Mom the other night. (Pretty *not* insane):

So, I went to my front door and opened it wide. There stood my enraged Mom in the hallway. She was dressed in her hospital paraphernalia with little tubes and hoses attached to her body. You ask about deranged, you should have taken a gander at her.

"Mom" I said, "We have to get you back to Mount Sinai, you're very sick - and you look terrible ..."

She interrupted me with, "Don't you Mount Sinai me, you little, you little shit, piss, traitor creep ..." She always interrupted me when I spoke. She would never let me finish a sentence. I hate that.

Then Mom noticed the rats, the hundred fifty or so rats, rapturously looking at Julie Andrews as they listened to her while she was humming the Epais Dorme, Flower Duet.

"What the good goddamned hell is going on in here? This is revolting..." She was gasping. This is when I gave a signal to Julie Andrews for her to change the tune to the Tupac Shakur number, the one that drives the rats mad. You want insane, you should see them writhe to Tupac.

"Oh, Oh, Oh..." Mom was at a loss for words. A rare moment. It was delicious. And as the rats were turfing and stomping in her direction, with their little sharp teeth showing in a most hostile manner, Mom clutched her right forearm with her left hand. I had been of the impression when you had a heart attack you grabbed at your heart towards the middle of your chest, like they do in the movies - but such is not always the case. Mom went "Oh, Oh," a few more times. Then she slid to the floor. Julie Andrews down-shifted to the Epais Dorme, which effectively called off the rats.

I promptly carted Mom back to her room at the geriatric ward. I wanted her in her room and in bed because she was a good beard for my gaining entrance into Mathuzala's chamber, which is, as you will recall, located behind Mom's commode. I needed the Master's advice on many issues.

When I entered his sanctuary, Mathuzala was propped up, sipping on his fluids, "Ahh, there you are my little Pea-pod. I need you to do a little chore for me." Puff, Blow, Sip. "Cough, cough."

"Of course, Mathuzala, anything. But I have to have your advice, right now, on several matters."

"All my wisdom is your wisdom, Howsoever,"… (Note: Mathuzala, frequently would use the archaic form of a word, to remind you of better linguistic times, I suppose.) "…before I can be of assistance to you, I need you to buy me a carton of Luckies." (Note: Mathuzala, would only smoke Luckies – and they are getting harder and harder to find these days. But providing for Mathuzala's wishes is an insignificant quibble.)
"Mathuzala, you shouldn't smoke. It could kill you for goodness sake - any doctor will tell you that."

"Buy me the Luckies, or you will hear nothing. Chzleeck!" "Wheeze." I could tell he was deadly serious. His face puffed up and he scowled, "Your kind, in the name of science, addicted me to cigarettes. Then the sadistic lab-techs studied me in my withdrawal and took endless notes during my subsequent forced relapses. They learned much from those studies; published some results and buried others… and now…now I am going to smoke every gol-darned Lucky I can light up before I meet whoever the Maker is. Chleezk. (Cough, Cough.) Little Pea-pod, I am going to die soon - so let me enjoy myself."

You do not argue with Mathuzala. I did his bidding and went to the Korean Deli down on 96th street. I was stunned at the price of cigarettes these days. Who can afford them?

Anyway, once Mathuzala was hooked up with an apparatus on the left side of his neck so he could smoke at will - and after he had a couple of good deep drags, I gave him a quick debriefing of everything that had transpired since I saw him only hours ago:

- The death of the strange threatening man in Mom's bed.
- The meeting of Eloise - my heart.
- Red having a clandestine huddle with Mose & Err.
- Mom finding me at the Plaza, and the rats and Julie Andrews giving her a mild myocardial infarction.

A busy day, all in all.

I ended by saying "What we have here is a piquant, catastrophic, insane, mélange of bizarre, joyous and terrible life experiences, confluencing and collecting into either one solid perilous mass or deteriorating into raw destructive energy- which is which or what is what, I do not know." I was almost teary." (I try to use important words when I talk to Mathuzala. I want to impress him as much as I can, knowing he does not suffer fools gladly.) Telling Mathuzala all this caused me to rub my temples so hard I gave myself a headache.

"Ahh, my Little Pea-pod." Mathuzala said. He took another drag and then: He fell into a deep, deep sleep.

At first, I could not believe he had deserted me in my time of need, I was completely alone in my garden of toil. I could feel my pulse rate pumping up. I massaged my forehead and kneaded one wrist with one hand and then the other wrist with the other. I did some New Age Shakti Gawain breathing exercises and managed to get my heart rate under control.

In short order, I could see with great clarity: Mathuzala was up there in the Cloud, the great I-Cloud, roaming over the millions of trillions of bits of information forming that enormous Cumulus Nimbus Gigantean I-Cloud. Mathuzala was condensing and 'packing' data and extracting exactly what it was I needed to carry on; to win the day.

It seemed like forever, but it was probably only a couple of minutes. I sat alone and waited for Mathuzala to wake, to come back to me. I changed his fluid pack and added a few more Luckies to his... his bong; I guess you would call it.

While I was sitting vigil, I heard strange voices coming from Mom's room on the other side of the toilet. I decided I better go out of Mathuzala's chamber and see what was going on near Mom's bedside. Before I exited her bathroom, I flushed the toilet, so nosey busybodies would think I had been doing my business in there; a deceptive maneuver. Crazy? I don't think so.

I entered Mom's room, pretending to cleanse my hands with one of those smelly sanitizers that everybody uses nowadays. It was then that I met the three guys from the Agency

How did I know they were from the Agency? Anybody who watches TV, or has seen a movie, knows what these guys look like. They do not flash badges; did you know that?

You do not have to speak to them. Did you know that, also? It is in the Constitution somewhere. But if you don't speak to them, you are in big trouble. Panic is the first emotion that runs through you when you see these corn-fed, rubber muscled guys, standing there, coming after you - even though you are the good guy.

'Whoa', I thought. *Be careful. 'HHHmmm'*, I thought, *'WWMD? What Would Mathuzala Do?'* I channeled Mathuzala, up there running around in the I-Cloud. And he helped. A calm came over me. I determined to be polite and conversant.

"Can I help you, sirs?"

End of Chapter 13

"DEXTER & FELIX"

Dexter & Felix are young and foolish. They laugh. They play. Their parents, knowing how innocent kids are, haven't let them to go up and out of the sewers in NYC. and see the disgusting things that go on above ground. Let kids be kids, for a while – they say.

CHAPTER 14

LEMON OR POMEGRANATE

The madness multiplies what with all the high techies and the mathematicians. It is not all ones and zeroes as the Algorithmics would have you believe. They think everything can be reduced to - and constructed by - Ones and Zeroes. Millions of billions of trillions of Ones and Zeroes explaining everything in the Cloud. They and you are wrong in this. There is more. There is a Two. I have seen it. And you will see: The Cloud is based upon a false assumption - and the errors will soon begin to rain down."

-Excerpted from: https://notesfromtheroomofwonder.com

. . . .

"What were you doing in the bathroom? You weirdo!" Yelled the one I call 'Curley', though he was shaved bald to a shiny spud head. They love this look, the Agency types. Bruce Willis made it popular.

Anyway, before I could speak, Moe, who looked as dumb as he was about to sound, broke in with the incredibly stupid, "You're talking to the Russkies in there, aren't you? We could hear your voice going on and on in there. Strange sounds. Foreign National noises. Who were you talking to? You traitor nerd-bastard."

'HHHmmm.' I was gob smacked to speechlessness. 'What on earth is going on?' I thought. 'Russkies? If these guys think I'm playing in yesterday's ballgame, they have another think coming.'

Mom. Mom is the only one I can think of who would have turned me in. Having had nothing else to do but lie around all day in her comatosed state, she probably heard my voice through the doors to Mathuzala's hide-away. She must have ratted me out - pardon my French. This had to be before she saw what was going on in my apartment, before she had any notion of what is truly coming down. *"Russkies?"* I thought. And I laughed out loud at the absurdity of the accusation. Which was a mistake because that is when Larry tasered me.

We humans learned how to tazer people by practicing first on rats. Did you know that? Tazers are *in*. The civilian control tool of choice. Thousands of rats lost their lives for the cause. Now a former mayor of New York and an off again candidate for President of the United States sells tazers for a living. He is making a killing. Anyway, Larry squeezed out a five second ride for me on his prongs and I flopped around, uncontrollably, on the floor. I was totally 'Decentralized'. The pain was excruciating. Oddly, you do not necessarily lose control of your sphincter muscles or bladder when on the ride. I am grateful for the small blessing.

The old bromide of 'If it does not kill you, it makes you stronger' is wrong, wrong, wrong - in the tazer instance. I felt weaker for the experience for days after. Weaker, with an aftertaste for a mite of revenge; but not stronger.

So, … I was, writhing around on the floor for I don't know how long after the tingling had stopped - and then, all of a sudden, I was dreaming of Eloise. Eloise and I, the two of us eating parfaits in the Palm Court. And Mathuzala. Mathuzala was in my reveries, too.

When I came to, I was in a twelve foot by twelve foot, white, whisper walled, blast proofed room. The three stooges had me seated up in a black chair with my left arm strapped in a blood-pressure air pad, which was blown up a little too tightly for my comfort, if you ask me. My right forefinger had a clamp on it and a wire ran from the clamp to the monitor Larry was looking into. There was also a wire running from the cushion upon which I was sitting to the black computer looking thing on Larry's desk. Larry was the only stooge in the room at that time. Bad cop, no good cop kind of interrogation.

"Try not to move," was Larry's greeting.

'O.K'. I said to myself, '*I can do that. I can try not to move. What's going on?*'

Larry looked into his screen, "We thought you would like to tell us the truth. Would you like to tell us the truth?"

"Who are you guys? What's going on?"

"We just want to know if you are violating National Security. If you are not violating the security of the United States of America, we will be on our way. We can finish this up in a couple of minutes. Or, we can take as long as it takes. Is there anything you want to tell us?"

Wait, if you don't believe me, I'll show you the transcripts...

(Some of our Chumpers are as good at hacking as ever there was. And remember, some of our fellow rodents now roam the data in the Cloud at will.)

The Poly -Transcript

Larry:

    "Is there anything you want to tell us?"

Me: **Truth   Lies**

    "What's this? Who are you guys? Where am I?"

                                       bp = 120/70

Larry:

    "You are hooked up to a polygraph. This is a highly tuned, scientific, state of the art device - which will tell us if you are telling us the truth. If you have nothing to hide, there should be no problem. Shall we move on?"

(I remember having had the sensation of channeling Mathuzala at that instant 'Tell them the truth', he was saying. 'They won't believe you anyway. The truth will not make sense to them. They will only understand it when it is too late. Tell them the truth.')

	Truth	Lies

Me:

"O.K. Let's move on. Give it your best shot.

My left arm is killing me. The band is vel-cro'd too tightly."
(Larry did not seem to care.)

bp = 120/70

Larry:

"Have you taken any drugs today? Any drugs that might cause you to be calmer than normal? Anything which might give us an inaccurate reading of your normal heart rate?"

	Truth	Lies

Me:

"No. I was tasered, though. That might affect your readings…"

bp = 125/78

Larry: *(…showing no reaction to my comments)*

"Have you taken any courses or programs which are intended to help you deceive a polygraph machine?"

Me: Truth   Lies

"No! What a question. You tasered ||\\|_____
me and brought me to who knows
where to ask me such a stupid
question? ... Don't they teach you
how to do these things right?"
                                             bp = 130/85

Larry:

"Just reply with a 'Yes' or 'No' And
don't move. You are twitching.
Why are you twitching? Is there
something you want to tell us?"

Me: Truth   Lies

"How do I tell you about my
twitching with a Yes or No? And |||
the answer to your question is   bp = 135/90
'No'. No there is nothing I want to
tell you. Does your machine tell
you I'm telling you the truth? Or
what?"

Larry: *(Not responding, looking only into
          his screen.)*
          "Let's start with a test. We'll ask
          you to lie. Lie to this question.
          Here is the question: A lemon is a
          pomegranate. Do you agree?"

                                             Truth   Lies

Me:

"You guys are nuts. What are you   _____
talk-..."

                                             bp = 137/95

Larry:

"...A lemon is a pomegranate. Do you agree?"

Me:

"Yes"   Truth   Lies

(Pause. Larry makes a mark on a   _____|__
piece of paper with a pencil.)

                                bp = 139/96

Larry:

"Now I want you to tell me the truth to the following question: A lemon is a pomegranate. Do you agree?"

Me: Truth   Lies

"What on earth -"

                                _____

Larry: bp = 140/99

"Do you agree?"

Me: "No."   Truth   Lies

(Larry makes a pencil mark. He
takes his folder and leaves the room. _|_____
Five minutes later, Moe enters and bp = 140/99
sits behind the truth machine. He
makes a few adjustments to some
knobs and then, without looking
at me...)

Moe:

"Have you been in contact with any foreign nationals?"

Me: Truth   Lies

"Ever? What is this? Foreign nationals? What…"

_____

Moe: bp= 150/105

"Just answer the question. Are you in contact with any foreign nationals?"

Me: Truth   Lies

"No. And you changed the question. You guys are not very good at this, are you?"

_||_____

bp = 160/107

Moe:

"Why are you so excited? And stop moving in the chair. You will affect the readings.
…Do you want to tell me something?"

Me: Truth   Lies

"No. I do not want to tell you ||\\|_____
anything - but I will tell you   bp = 150/110
everything. All you have to do is
ask the right questions."

Moe:

"Have you joined any groups of religious fanatics or foreign nationals who want to overthrow the United States?"

Me:

"No! Never!"   **Truth   Lies**

(And, as you can see, that was the ||**|_____
god's honest truth.)

bp = 160/115

And so it went for over two hours. Moe came into the sweat-box and told me I was lying. He said the machine told them I was lying, which I knew was a lie of his own. Moe said if I came clean and told them I had made a mistake and that I had given secrets to, or, helped foreign nationals plot against the United States they would go easy on me. Now was the time, he said.

I said the machine was broken. Moe sneered condescendingly to me and said the machine was not broken and the Chief Polygrapher had tested the machine earlier that day and it was in good working order. I told Moe to bring the Chief Polygrapher in and I would tell *him* his machine was broken and we went round and round and about and I never cracked and I never lied and they never asked about the rats and if they had I would have told them everything. ...And they would have looked at the results on their stupid high-tech charts and they would have thrown the lie-detector into the dumper and gone back to square one.

Moe, Curley and Larry let me go, but they told me they were going to keep an eye on me. I made a mental note to have a combination locked, four hundred-pound fireproof, bomb resistant door put on the entrance to Mom's bathroom - and another one leading to Mathuzala's room. I made another note to go to the Spy Store and buy every bug-proof device known to man.

I also made a note to see if Red, or some rat could drop a little something in the food of one of those stooges - just to get a little payback for the tasering and the five second ride.

End of Chapter 14

"INGRID"

Ingrid has recently emerged from the open drainpipe on 57th & Lex. She desperately wants to cross the street to see what scraps are available on the other side. Not only does she have to look up, but also left and right to watch to avoid traffic. Life will be easier when there are no cars.

CHAPTER 15

THE CORN HOARDER

"The pendulum is swinging back. Any fool can see that. But does the fool notice the pendulum is swinging back proportionally further than from whence it came? And when the momentum reverses the next time, the pendulum will go further, past the other extreme. The big stick is moving faster and harder and the pin looks break..." (Puff, Blow, and Sip) ..."And all this turbulent commotion is for what? So, humans can eat tasty meats? Is it for their temporary, sensory entertainments? For their streamings, movies, games, apps, phones, guns and toys? ... (Puff, Blow, Drag, Cough.) "Or is it so they can obey the interpreted dictations from their various gods? For what? The whole pendulum could go flying off and if that were to happen it would be by-by to everything before you even notice the fulcrum is being tested...Just look at the weather, and follow the riots the world over, and observe the Great Poisonings, ...and the Massive Starvations ... and the Extinctions - do you follow them? The Extinctions? ... (Cough) This is why we must act now."

-Excerpted from: https://notesfromtheroomofwonder.com

• •

Eloise handed me the obnoxious note which the Plaza's concierge had given to her. (Everybody around here knows about Eloise and me - which is fine by me.) The note was from my editor, who I am about to fire. It read, "Really, Mr. Benedict, you must add some action - or no reader will bother to finish reading your story. And if no one wants to finish reading your story - then I am afraid we will have to take a pass on this project"...

signed, Yours Truly, ... etc. & blah de dee blah....And then she affixed the p.s. (always the most important part of any message): "And DO NOT EVER AGAIN PLANT ANYMORE OF YOUR RAT DROPPINGS IN MY OFFICE!!! Your practical jokes are not appreciated. I am beginning to think you have a sick mind."

Well, if my being tasered, jailed and then polygraphed aren't enough 'action' for the 'Dear reader'... or, how about my pulling the plug on my mother's lover? (Yes, that is what I suspect him to have been. The creep. He was taking advantage of her in her sickly state. Some would call what I did 'murder' But who is to blame me for protecting my own mother? I should have told you my thoughts on this earlier. My bad.)

If all this is not enough thrilling titillation for you, well, then you can go pick up some piece of the mind rotting sex-capade, serial killer drivel which is being published and peddled on 'Best Seller' commercial lists nowadays. Anyway, I have no choice over when action starts, or how much of it there is.

Hang in there. Turbulence is about to come around the corner. But, if you are a well-balanced human, you are not going to like it. As for the rat droppings, I did not know what the editor was referring to.

Without going into intimate details, Eloise and I have become an 'item'. She was completely understanding about my relationship with the rats. As a matter of fact, Eloise became a 'Chumpette' on her very first official meeting with them. The rats adored her. What's not to adore? They had never met an Eloise Impersonator before - and not just any Eloise Impersonator but the world's very best.

Eloise has moved in with me and we have given her apartment over to a cadre of rats so they can hold political meetings, dancings, propagatings and other activities which accommodate their movement's needs. We liked to call our little group of Red, Petal, Julie Andrews, Eloise, and me: 'The Ratical Chic'. It was fun; but the fun did not last long.

Let us go back to the night I returned to my apartment after the grilling from the Three Stooges.

Red, Petal and Julie Andrews were on my terrace. Julie Andrews was in a funky mood. Lately, she had taken to incessantly singing songs which reflected what was on her mind or which emotions she was feeling. She was forever singing now, even if it was just a little louder than under her breath. Maybe it was to hide her speech defect. She would sing a well-known song which indicated her thoughts of the situation at hand. This night, for example, Julie Andrews was humming "There ss a Bad Moon on the Rise", the Fogerty smash hit. You know the one. I remember hoping she had not turned into one of those creepy people who could foretell things. Or fore*sing*, in her case. "Bad Moon on the Rise" is a great song, and if you have to go down - well, it's a good number to go down to.

As for Red, she was not her usual beautiful, snarling, threatening self. She appeared distraught and vulnerable - as if she were about to burst into tears. Petal was at Red's ankle, cute as ever, but quivering, uncontrollably.

"What? What's going on?" I asked, with some trepidation, for this had not been a good patch I had been going through recently; and I suspected my bad bio-rhythms had not exhausted themselves.

Red blurted out, "Oh, Bene," (By the way, that is pronounced:'Bay-Nae', like the Italian.) "Err has betrayed us...He is a monster. A monster." And then she broke into sobs. "What are we going to do?" she was asking me. Me? As if I were some kind of a take charge kind of a guy. *Why me?* I thought. Who am I to lead in these difficult times? Readers of history know all great leaders have these moments of doubt.

My first flash in a millisecond of a thought was: 'What do you mean *we*? Kemo Sabe?' But this was no time for jokes, so I stifled it and said, "What? What on Earth are you talking about?" I had the sickening feeling the conversation I recently had with the Three Stooges would stack up as a less painful experience than the one I was about to have.

Cutting through Red's hysterics, below is a condensed brief of what she had to tell me. (If you are interested to know these things: Red has a deep voice, reminiscent of Marlene Dietrich's in tone. She uses proper Rat grammatical structure, which reveals a fine upbringing...For example, her 'cheek' sounds more like 'cheeck' – it is a subtle differentiation; but the cultivated ear can hear the deep South, perhaps Savanna. She speaks an English/Rat patois - which I have translated into solid American. I have deleted her sobs but retained some of her 'Cheecks' to give you the flavor her message.)

"It started to fall apart a few days ago...Petal and I were working on the stage in the upper sub-basement...setting up for Mose & Err's next city-wide video presentation to the rats and Chumpers...when I accidentally bumped up against an old door, which has not been used for many years. The door opened a crack and...cheeck...and cheeck...I was looking into a small room, maybe 20' by 20'...It must have been a janitor's room long ago....and, and in the center of the room was a large pile of corn. Yes, corn. Piled almost to the ceiling. Cheeck. And on top of the pile of corn... bloated from gorging and completely passed out - was Err.

"Bene, Err is not what he seems. Not what he preaches...CHEECK ..." (Red's integrating the cheecks into her vocabulary is a sign of her having gone 'native', as it were. This sort of thing happens; people pick up speaking patterns of those they associate closely with. I am not that far gone.) "... Err has broken with the rats' natural code of living for the swarm,' all for the pack, and the pack for all'...Bene, Err is amassing personal property! Cheeck. Err is in it for himself...he is no better than a greedy, gluttonous human. ... And the corn hoarding; disgusting! Maybe it has something to do with those opposing thumbs of his, I don't know. I don't care..."

Poor Petal. She, too, was distraught. The little rodent rubbed her nose against Red's ankles and whimpered in sympathy for her big human friend.

I must interrupt at this point. Red, you see, was 'in it' for idealistic purposes. Not like most of us, who were collecting our own corn, if you will. Red really wanted to believe the rats were of a higher order.

Mathuzala had warned me: "Corruption leads to power - and absolute corruption leads to absolute power. (Cough.)" Mathuzala was right, of course - and Red had deduced that Mose & Err were corrupt. She was mightily upset. Her fingernails nails raked the flesh of her forearms so hard that they bled. She pulled frantically at her hair, ripping tufts of it from her scalp. It was not an attractive sight, watching Red losing it.

I could see a shift in the balance of power in that Red was not going to do the bidding of Mose & Err anymore. Such is the way with idealists.

Events were in flux, again. That could be a good thing – *if only we can get from here to there*. 'HHHmmm', I tried to think.

Back to Red's debriefing:

"Petal and I found the video-agenda for the upcoming 'Chumpers' Spectacular' and in it we saw that Mose & Err were going to call for immediate action, action against the humans...

"'It was time.' according to the script Err had prepared and was going to broadcast ...CHEEK...'Time to avenge the recent hideous attack against the Rat population in New York City'..."

What recent attack? I thought. '*HHHmmm.*'

"Bene, we, cheeck, Petal and I..." and poor Petal was shaking with fear, her eyes bulging wide. "...we saw the proof - only an hour ago: first the video-pictures of over one hundred thousand rats, dead rats, who had been poisoned in the sub, sub-lower basement of the Plaza. ...Their bodies in horrible, agonized, contorted positions. ...and then we found them in the sub-sub-basement, the poor dead critters down there, cheeck ...and we know the humans had nothing to do with this. ...Err and his troops did it and, cheeck... they did it with the intention of blaming the massacre entirely on the humans...who would gladly have done the same deed, but they did not do it this time...and, and Err did this to advance his own cause...to seize power...and, oh Bene, I am afraid this horrible lie is being '*leaked out*' as the truth.

"...Never before has a rat so much as *lied* to another rat, cheeck... never...and not knowing what a lie is: rodents, believe in their hearts that this ugly story told to them is the truth ... cheeck...and now rodents of all kinds are moving to Manhattan to see...to see, cheeck, what is next on Err's program. ...To see what they, the rodents can do. ...chee-eeeck...And when I say rodents, I don't mean just rats...The porcupines are coming. Nutrias coming up from the swamps. Rodents of all kinds leaving the estuaries, marshes and wetlands. Beavers, Marmots, Muskrats...and their cousins, the Voles and the Shrews, all who feel they have a vested interest in the outcome."...

You get the picture. Err had started his own violent terrorist cell - and it was metastasizing. He was plotting to grow outside the Chumpers' modality. He was not going to wait for a slow evolution of *the movement* for the awakening of the animals to take the dominion away from the humans. None of this 'Start a revolution and the leaders will follow' for Err. No sir, Err would be the leader of the sect from the get-go. El Jefe, The Big One, The Capo di Capi. When I said Err, I meant to leave Mose out. For Red had fathomed, correctly, that Mose was truly a moron of a rat, (who, by the way, had been lobotomized a year ago by an experiment at the Rockefeller Institute) - but who happened to look like one heck of a wise rat. A rat, rats would follow because of his wise looks. Err had been using Mose as a prop all along. Mose had not even been invited to gaze into the Corn Hoard room.

Trying to digest this humongously negative portentous report, our little group of Ratical Chic fell silent, except for Julie Andrews' humming of "How High is the Water Mama?" A Johnny Cash classic.

And then came the worst of it. Petal gave a pathetic whimper and a violent spasm - and then she died right in front of us. She just rolled over and died.

Red shrieked so loud she could have been heard on the uptown side of Central Park. Her grief was deep and extreme; never to be abated. There was sweat and blood and anger - and more to come.

Julie Andrews was so dumbstruck no song came to mind.

Poor Petal was there; but gone. We were at a miserable, wretched loss.

The little rat must have eaten some of the food which had poisoned the other rats in the sub, sub-basement.

A scheming human once noted: "The death of One is a Tragedy. The death of a Hundred Thousand is a statistic." For the rats, however, there is a different insight: The death of one rat is a tragedy. The death of a hundred thousand rats is an even greater tragedy.

It looked like Err was getting what he wanted: A great variety of rodents were on their way to the City to pay their respects.

End of Chapter 15

"MAX"

Max watched Pammy do the Cha-Cha Electric Slide and he fell in love. Since then, the two got hitched and have had over two hundred babies.

CHAPTER 16

PASTEL

"Trust no one. Not even yourself."
-Excerpted from https://notesfromtheroomofwonder.com

∙∙∙

Look what I found while I was hacking around: an e-mail. An e-mail from the General Pool of Knowledge:

From: Andy Prog. I-Tech, NYC Dept. of Environment
Date: July 8 (Time: 1:28 P.M.)
To: Emily Hoarst, Admin. Dir., NYC Dept. of Environment
Subject: Rats in the sewers

Emily,

Two things:

1) It has come to my attention there are reports of over a hundred thousand rats, dead rats, clogging our sewer system - especially affecting the underground channels from the mid-town area leading to the filtration plants by the West Side Drive. We do not know the cause of this; but it can't be all bad news. Perhaps we should PR the situation and claim it is a result of some pest control measures we have taken. This could be an assist in our asking for

an increase in our annual budget - the review of which comes up in a few months.

I'd like your feedback on this at your earliest.

2)   Drinks and a meet tonight at O'Neal's? Ladies half price.

Andy

From: Emily Hoarst, Amin. Dir., NYC Dept of Environment
Date: July 8, (1:28.5 P.M.)
To: Andi Prog, I-Tech, NYC Dept. Of Environment
Subject: O'Neal's
Andy,

1)   I'll be there with bells on.
2)   What is this about Rats in the gutters? Are you at O'Neal's already? Leave some for the rest of us.

Emily.

Wait, here is another:

From: Jim Broadcraft, Freelance Reporter/New York Post
Date: July 8 (2:12 P.M.)
To: Alan Judelson, Editor, City Desk, New York Post
<u>Subject: Rats in the City</u>

Alan, I have it on good authority there is an epidemic of some sort which is killing thousands, maybe even hundreds of thousands of rats in the City. Will you authorize payment for me to check this out and write the story? ...it could be big. BIG. We are talking scoop. ...Scooop.

Hurry, Jimmy

...And back:
From: Alan Judelson, Editor, City Desk, New York Post

Date: July 8 (2:12:30 P.M.)
To: Jim Broadcraft, Freelance Reporter/New York Post
Subject: <u>Rats in the City...NO Authorization NO!!!</u>

Jimmy, Rats in the City is an old story and does not sell papers. Baseball scores, sex, murder, corruption ...that's what sells papers and that's what we want and that's what we pay you for. A word from the wise: It is 'Mr. Judelson' to you. See company memo on 'e-mail protocol'. A. K. Judelson, Editor, City Desk

I retrieved many such correspondences relating to the assault by Err upon the Plaza's rats. The point is: Every bit of information was there to be had and appreciated, right at the earliest inception of the rat movement against the era of : "The Humans' Dominion of The Animals and The Earth." But the humans refused to take it in. What is the advantage of having all that information at our fingertips if we never put it to good use? What? Tell me.

Back to the story.

Our little group of Ratical Chic, minus Petal, retreated to Mathuzala's bedside redoubt. God forgive me, I brought him another carton of Luckies. He made smoking look quite enjoyable, I must say.

While Mathuzala heard the details about Err having killed his own rats, tears streaked down the whiskers on his grizzled cheeks. After our recounting, the room fell silent for a long while. Complete silence, except for the sounds of the occasional sip, a few coughs and the deep drags from a Lucky. The room was a cloudy mist from the blowings of medicated air and exhaled smoke from out of our tiny dear Leader's puffed up jowls.

"I'll be back in a moment. Cheeck," Mathuzala said in a saddened and distant voice. Then he closed his eyes and went to the cloud.

The rest of us sat there in a sullen quiet for I do not know how long. We were full of fear. What could *we* do? Who were *we to survive* this course, let alone change the direction of the flow? I was afraid whatever we would come up with might result in a stragedy. (My word, I invented it out of thin air. 'Stragedy'; give me credit.)

The tempo had picked up.

First, there was an exciting new movement. Then before you knew it, a power grabbing sect arises. And what were we? A troubadouring power singer. An angry, passionate causista. A super I-tech (Me). An Eloise impersonator. And not a rat amongst us, if you don't count Mathuzala. How could we depend upon him? He was gone from us, roaming over all the digitized knowledge ever recorded.

Suddenly his eyes opened wide.

"Light me another, little Peapod." Anything. I would do anything for him. I affixed a new Lucky to his hookah. After a few drags he spoke.

"Come up hither." We scrunched our chairs up close to the bed to hear what Mathuzala had learned from his journey.

"I have learned: 'If you think you see things clearly, look again.'"

"For example, I have found among the trillions of bits in the cloud that the scientists have recreated Spanish Flu in the labs. And why? Why recreate the Spanish flu? So, you can create a five-billion-dollar pill to cure the Flu in case it breaks out, or is leaked out?... Maybe. But the deep answer to 'Why?' is: Because the madness has multiplied. The madness is on the Fibonacci curve which is spiraling in its ascent. The results will be incalculable.

..."So, if you think you see the answer clearly, you are being deceived. For nothing is clear. Look again. Whatever you and I believe and know - odds are we are wrong. The only good news is: So is everybody else. Believe that. Know this. You can only do what you can do. And that may not be enough. But there you have it.

"I have come to see: When the lion feeds, he is most vulnerable. And right now, there are two beasts at the trough. Err is on the feed - and so is the human race. And both entities are most vulnerable at this juncture - right here and now - though, to the idle viewer that would seem counter-intuitive.

"...Neither Err, nor the humans are friends of ours. Yet both are enemies to each other. Enemies of our enemies are not our friends; they are still our enemies. Only friends and friends of our friends are our friends." (Drag, Buff, blow "Chleeczk" "Cough, cough" Wheeze.)

"*HHHmmm*," I thought. Mathuzala's pain-killers must have been over-prescribed. Here we have a surging, immediate life- threatening situation on our plate and our leader has gone adrift speaking in un-understandables and re-examining platitudes. (I must admit, I have re-read his words several times - since that wondrous meeting - and the more I ponder over, these utterances of Mathuzala, the more I learn. However, in our hour of need, his fevered rattling seemed like so much dreck.

Mathuzala looked at us and waited for his wisdom to permeate through our tiny, semi-diffusible membranes. He smoked another cigarette.

A minute passed.

"I have sent for help." (Puff, Blow, Sip)

Relief.

"What? Who?" This from Red; but she asked for our entire clique.

And Mathuzala spoke thus, "You know I was the subject of several experiments on Plum Isle. I was the unwilling participant in a study which related to the development of the mind. You see, the scientists knew man's brain had evolved a good deal since he first walked the earth, some one million two hundred and forty-four thousand years ago. ...But, oddly, his *mind* had not progressed a nit. The scientists wanting to explore that issue, planted beta and protein enhancers under my amygdala in hopes of expanding my mind. The operation was labeled: PASTEL # 1. Chzeelck. Probably because the serum injected in my brain was Crayola crayon green in color. (Not very imaginative, but scientists rarely are.) I endured two pastel green injections just before the raid from PETA, which closed the place down. The scientists never benefitted from the fruits of their work on me. Not only did my brain grow exponentially, but my mind grew at warp speed and is today one of the most penetrating minds in the known Universe. That explains why whatever I say is so wise and clever. When I say 'one of the most penetrating minds' I am not being modest - for there are others who are extant, others with greater minds than mine. They are descendants of mine.

"I have been busy since my escape from the now defunct and nefarious Plum Isle. Children, grandchildren - all with enlarged craniums. Separate, or together, they are a dynamic force of nature. I did not wish for them a life where they would have to enter this fray - but they must. Chlzeeclk! It is time."

And at that precise moment a little rat with an enormous head popped out of the air register located down at the floor, next to Mathuzala's bed. Then came another and another and so on. Upon seeing them, Julie Andrews clapped her hands with joy and broke into her version of "Go Ask Alice" - the smash hit originated by Grace Slick and the Jefferson Airplane. "One pill makes you bigger and one pill makes you small"... You know the one.

Red smiled for the first time ever since I knew her. She gave a quick flash of both her shiny pointy canines. My guess is going up against lions, who were pigging out at the trough picked up her spirits. It is hard to keep a good woman down.

Eloise? Eloise was just a delight to behold - as she was dexterously playing an imaginary game of hopscotch in the far corner of the room.

End of Chapter 16

"MO"

Do not be deceived! Mo is much cleverer than he looks. Right now, he's watching Eloise play hopscotch and knows he can do it even better – on the first try.

CHAPTER 17

QUICK

"You are drinking and drugging all over the map. You are addicted to your 'medicines' and are feeding each other cancerous foods. You are diminishing your gene pools, destroying your brain cells and lessening your abilities to think reasonably. What is that all about?" (Puff, Blow, Sip & Drag) "No rats would behave like that - except in experiments...."
- https://notesfromtheroomofwonder.com

•••

Mathuzala's progeny are a formidable crew. In many ways they have become what we should have been, could have been. They are physically healthy, of sound mind, and emotionally stable. They are way up high on the Aristotelian Triangle, climbing towards 'Pure Being' (The closest some of us come to this state is when we do a 'Personal Best in some sport or gaming activity – no comparison, really.) Of course, I am not saying we should become like four-legged scavenging rodents, but these rats in particular are something special and I am the better for knowing them.

Let me digress a moment from our story and wax on a little more about Mathuzala. Everybody should be so lucky as to have such a creature in their life. If you were to stay with Mathuzala long enough, you, too, would become a wise one. Like me. You may have noticed as my tale progresses, I seem wiser, cleverer and more adept at handling situations which would baffle and confuse a more normal person. Mathuzala is responsible for all this.

I have told you before, you can access his wisdom blog for free ('free'

105

means 'no money') and in time you could become smarter than you had ever hoped to be. All Mathuzala's postings are for the human readers' benefit – as his offspring already share his knowledge. I'm not advising you whether or not to become a Chumper. I'm just saying you ought to do yourself a favor and look into it – see if it is good for you.

There is a religious sect in India which believes when a Wise-Man dies; he comes back as a rat - which is why this age- old cult never eats rats.

Tangentially, I hope when Mathuzala does die and then comes back – that he comes back as a Wise-Man. He once told me that in the Great Wheel of Recurring Spinning he was supposed to have come back *this* time, in this present life, as a Wise-Man; but something got screwed up, up there with the allocations and he came down as the rat he is. All this notwithstanding, we can use him right now in any form. He is of tremendous help in addressing the oncoming human counter-insurgency problems. But I'm getting ahead of my story. Besides, if he had come back here as a Wise-Man we'd probably have killed him, if history has anything to do with the current events.

Returning to the Progeny, who I named the Ma-STERs (A hybrid acronym for: Mathuzala's Scientists, Technicians, Engineers and Rationalizers - the s is for plural). They revered me. Why? I'm not absolutely certain, but I think it has something to do with my having given Mathuzala safe quarters, been his first human disciple and having established myself, selflessly, as the intermediary between the rats and the human race.

Let me tell you something I have learned; a truth, if you will. You have heard it is lonely at the top? Well, I have been up there, and *it is* lonely there, but it is *lonelier* at the bottom, even though it is more crowded. I know, because I've been there too. You will agree with me, that good leadership comes from the ground up.

Of course, they can speak English, the Ma-STERs. In fact, they speak many languages and are even fluent in Esperanza, Some say it will become the Lingua Franca of the human race - *if* we survive the After Bacci Era. These troopers are ahead of the curve; speaking a language which does not exist is quite something.

Back to where I left off;
The Ma-STERs seamlessly took control of Mathuzala's room as soon

as they entered. You take one look at them and you know right off they are rats, but they have these disproportionately large heads. I guess that is to accommodate their enlarged brain casing. If F.A.O. Schwartz were inclined to sell a lovable stuffed animal of a rat, this would be it. They are so cute you want to pick one up and hug it. But their being so smart could be a little off-putting to the person with an average intellect. Personally, I find it intimidating to hug someone, or something, I feel inferior to, don't you? These adorable creatures can look into our eyes and through that look, they can understand what we are thinking. It is a remarkable facility, in all probability derived from our nefarious experiments concerning empathy, clairvoyance and pain. (Most of the experiments on rats contained an element of pain. The testings the rats are currently doing on the humans down in the sub, sub, sub-basement, are infused with a zero tolerance for pain, so I am assured.)

So, ...There we were, in Mathuzala's chambers, the Ratical Chic, looking at our new allies. The Ma-STERs took immediate command of the situation.

The Ma-STERs told Red, "Fear Not. You are a believer in our cause, and you will be safe, of good use and highly valued." Red was visibly relieved - she was locked in place - a recommitted acolyte.

They told Julie Andrews they admired her singing powers and they would give her, her biggest stage yet - and, also, they had a long list of songs to show her. Songs she could add to her quiver.

Best of all, I was informed I was 'The One'. I had suspected early on in my life that I was 'The One' - but as time droned on, I was beginning to lose faith that anybody else would figure it out. Yes, it was the Ma-STERs who put me on top - as the Leader of the Neo-Humanistic Movement. I was to be the leader of all the Chumpers. It was determined my leadership was to last six years, and I would be forbidden to seek another term. After the six years (which are not yet up) I was to be cast out of the Chumper movement and to descend to the lowly position of a normal human - a simple citizen of the earth. Thence, I would experience the trickle down, if you will, of the benefits, or the lack thereof, of my works for the Human Race. You have to admit, these Ma-STERs had thought it all out. (I will still be rich, they allowed me that. That counts for something, being rich.)

At the time, six years seemed a long way away and I was not bothered by the deal.

As for my love Eloise, the Ma-STERs told her if she were to purchase a tiny tea set, they would have tea with her in the afternoons.

The Ma-STERs are great record keepers (If you are any kind of a student of history, you will have noticed all the great super-powers were ardent record keepers). Below are three leaked classified dispatches from the early files of the

Ma-STERs:

Dispatch: "We have nibbled the fiber optic wiring and successfully disabled the mechanisms of the big broadcast Mose & Err were scheduling to all the Chumpers' Chapters. The show is unbroadcastable and cancelled."

Dispatch: "The Great Rodent Migration to the City has been discouraged for the time being. The Voles, Nutrias, Muskrats, Possums and so forth, have turned around and headed for from whence they came."

(How did they do this you may ask? It has something to do with their telepathic swarm powers. Why does it bother you? ...Your not understanding how this is done? You, who do not know how those little people appear in your Television screen at night, yet you believe it works. Go with this. The rodents turned around - all as one.)

Dispatch: "Err is detained in his corn hoarder room. The corn hoard has been removed and distributed to the rats in the neighborhood, freely given to the rats who survived the deposed leader's internecine, murderous poisonings. Err is looking at a small plate piled with what looks like the same poisoned food he fed his own kind." (The reason the food only 'looks like the same poisoned food' that Err used in his dastardly deed is because the Ma-STERs would never poison a fellow rat as they do not condone capital punishment of their own kind.)

The question at that time was: Would Err eat the food, thinking it was the easy way out of his shame? Would he choose to be among the quick or the dead? The betting odds were: Two to one, he eats it. You have to give the rat credit; he did not take the bait and he stood in the dock at his trial and spoke in his own defense, spewing venom about the human race and how the rodents needed someone strong like him to lead them into battle. The jury did not take long and The Ma-STERs, banished Err to the 'Middle of Nowhere', somewhere in Utah, or the like, and has never been heard from to this day.

As for Mose, he was returned to the company of the survivors of the pack in the basement, where he finished out his days with no one paying any mind to whom (who?) he had been.

We Chumpers were informed we had to be reprogrammed a bit, de-contaminated from the Mose & Err experience. A cleansing was in the offing, the purging would be mild - it was promised; but we were to be kept in place. So said our Ma-STERs.

It all seemed good after that first meet. The Ratical Chic was much encouraged.

End of Chapter 17

"OSCAR"

Oscar is one happy rat. He has no fears about tomorrow and no regrets about the past. There is a ripped open bag of garbage on the sidewalk on East 9th Street. What could be better? Who knew it would be so much fun to be a rat?

CHAPTER 18

TEARS...

"Once upon a time, a Persian king by the name of Xerxes thought he was so mighty he could reverse the tide. He was wrong. Present day world leaders and powerful corporate chieftains think they, too, can play the oncoming tide. It is all ebb and flow, they think. ... But it is not ebbing anymore. ... It is only coming on. It is cocking and jamming and getting ready. Add to all that: The ozone loss (Remember the 'ozone holes'?) has caused water vapors to move upwards. ... Now there are storms high in the Atmospheric reaches, which are usually drier than the deserts. The rains have started way up above without much notice, the results of which are disconcerting. For starters, there is a place in Australia bigger than Texas which flooded over only a short while back. In the U.S., rivers, lakes, and oceans, even, have crested over lands which never have seen water before - and this is not just along the Mississippi, but in places like the New York Stock Exchange, if you would believe. The TV has started to notice...but ratings for this sort of reality are low and the people are remoting to other channels. They do not want to know. It may be the beginning of the end for the humans. This will not be the much sought-after Apocalypse. Oh, no. My travels tell me their Savior is not coming with the big umbrella and the Anti-Christ does not like the climate either. It kind of tears at your heart, sometimes, to think about this. Maybe the humans will die out before they kill off all the other species, maybe not. But left to their own devices they will use their last bullet and the last bomb in the world's arsenals before they call it quits. And that is a problem." -Excerpted from: https://notesfromtheroomofwonder.com

The Ma-STERs had concluded Chumpers were vital to their mission, which was to bring about the New Order before the humans knew there was even a New Order in place. Recruitment became top priority. The Ma-STERs knew they needed educated and motivated Chumpers to properly fill their role. Up to this point in time many Chumpers were in it only for the money. Money was important, yes, but the Ma-STERs wanted to inculcate proper learning and obtain true believers. It was education, they thought, which would result in loyalty, dedication, and a sense of righteousness. Evangelical enthusiasm. And that is a possible chink in their armor - for nowhere does it show an educated citizenry has the GPS to Utopia.

So. We entered a period of re-learning for the Chumpers old guard and intense training for the new acolytes. Now don't get all huffy and say, "How could you? How could you subject yourself to - to *thought control?*" Well, it was not exactly like that. Besides, we humans have a long history of proven success with being indoctrinated. Tens of millions of Chinese have had successful thought purifying. Decades of millions of Russians, too, had their mental purges. So did the Vietnamese. Re-education they called it. And us - Americans, too. Yes, we Americans - who say we are programmed to believe we can solve any problem whenever we need to, whenever our back is to the wall. We were taught - and we *know* we are a uniquely smart, healthy, freedom loving, happy, and a wholesome family cherishing people. Brainwashing if you ask me. Just saying.

Anyway, all the Chumpers were sent to get their Ma-STERs degree. This was not kindergarten stuff like Bacci and Mose & Err taught with the mere re-arranging of the Ten Commandments. This was High Education - and in these classes, one had to be on top of one's game. The Chumpers were taught to the test. Here is an example of the kind of test they took (I might add, with a measure of pride, I was tasked, to help create the form of the test which you see below. p.s. I also proctored many of the first exams.):

Ma-STERS TEST No. 9 (REQUIRED)

Subject: <u>HUMAN STUDIES</u>

Instructions:

Answer each question by scratching over the scented patch, (**), located adjacent and to the left of your choice - and then follow the instructions as you are so directed. (Narrator's note: This test is graded by smell. Can you imagine? Scratch enough patches incorrectly and you flunk the smell test. Different times are coming, I tell you.)

Each question has a 'Best' answer. Scratch one only. The number of wrong answers will be subtracted from the correct. DO NOT GUESS. You have all the time in the world, if you answer correctly.

Begin.

#1) THE FIRST PROPOSITION:
Two billion humans are undernourished and cannot do manual labor. The human population will grow by 50% within five decades and food production will have to double in order to:
*Scratch below
If you choose
this answer

** a) Prevent failed states and subsequent increased terrorism. (If you choose this answer: Go to # 4)

** b) Maintain Big Agra corporate profits at a rate of 6% or more. This is a good thing. (If you choose this; Go to #5.)

** c) Meet minimum human nutritional requirements. This does not include the consideration of meat production. If humans insist on eating meat fifty years from now, food production will have to quadruple. ...and all the attendant antibiotics and fertilizers will need to expand in volumes exponentially. (Go to #7)

** d) There are too many people now; but in order to feed 9 billion of them: Per acre gains of bio-bushels would have to increase algorithmically. This may be good news for the likes of Monsanto and ADM, but the effluents from their factories is bad news for the rodents and other species. Therefor: The human population figure must be controlled. (Go to #6)

#2) You have not been instructed to read this paragraph. Learn to follow instructions and you will do well. Go to too many paragraphs you are not told to go to and you will be sent to the woman at the front of the room for re-mediation.

#3) Peace is undeclared war. During peace, there are no adversaries, no victories. It is hard to imagine winning in peacetime. So, when winning is the only and everything in a society...What comes next?

  **   a) You did it again. Though this paragraph may, or may not seem interesting to you, no one told you to read it. Too much of this and you fail the smell test. (Go back and read the instructions)

#4) Though this is true, it is not the 'Best 'answer. The New Order does not care about 'States' - failed, or otherwise. We are not concerned about human terrorism either, as long as those hoo-ha events are low-tech and not chemicalized.

(Examine all the answers before you scratch one off. *Think* about the best answer - *think as if you were a rat*.)

#5) Go see the woman at the front of the room with the word RED written over her left breast

#6) Right! Isn't it curious? You can go to any bookstore in America and you will not find one inch of books on the shelf dedicated to the subject of 'Population'. Not one inch. Humans do not want to know. Well, we know. The numbers must go down. You cannot afford civilization with your numbers as is. (Take a break. Go to the front of the room and have a bit of a dance with Julie Andrews who is doing the Cha-Cha slide. Then come back and go to # 8)

#7) This is true: but it is not the 'Best' answer. (Go back to paragraph #1 and put yourself in a rodent's frame of mind.)

#8) THE SECOND PROPOSITION:

The age of science is young - and it may never grow old. Your Science is not about truth. Your Science is about profits. Science is about patents and weaponizing. Many rodents and other animals have been and are killed in the name of Your Science. This must be atoned for and stopped.

The foregoing conclusion makes you:

** a) ...suspect this program does not bode well for your happiness. (If you chose this answer, go see RED, up front, for remediation exercises).

** b) ...realize despite all the good things Your Science has done for some of mankind: 15% of the world's population is disabled, 5% of the children are missing limbs, suffering from retardation or blindness or other such things...and as countries get richer from Your 'Scientific advancements', the Fast Food Industry (Which is people too), adores a vacuum, and rushes in, bringing with it diabetes and fat people and older people... and for what?

Look here, in India, which is joining this Global thingamajig, it is said they are bringing high tech porta-johns to many communities because it is too difficult for the elderly to crawl out to the tree line of the forest in order to poop.

And *people* squirm when they see rats. (Go to #10)

** c) ...want to watch an entertaining television show, or have a large bottle of beer, or maybe play a video game. Get away from it all, because who *are you* anyway? Less than one in a million, or worse, a billion. What can little *you* do? You're just one potato chip in the bowl. And what does all this have to do with you? You just want to be left alone. It is all too depressing. (Go to #9)

** d) ...you do not see what this has to do with becoming a Chumper - and you suspect it is a trick question. Or maybe you are taking the wrong test. Or are in the wrong room - like you are in that dream you have every once in a while. You would like to talk to the proctor in the pompadour because you think you may have missed a lecture or something. (Proctor's note: Yes, I was wearing a pompadour that day - as a disguise because I had seen Curly - remember Curly?...Well, he showed up out of the blue to be a Chumper and I did not want him to recognize me - until we determined whether or not he was sincere, or an undercover guy. Red had not sensed anything wrong with him on first whiff. But incognito was the wisest policy here. Thus, explaining the pompadour.)
(Go to # 12)

#9) True enough. But the wrong answer. Not the stuff of strong Chumper material! Get a grip on yourself, or you will lose it. Go back and try another scratch-off.

#10) BINGO! You are aware all the tools, gadgets, scientific and technological devices are nothing but job killers and the resultant high unemployment will cause unrest, strife, aggression, and even WAR...and you are beginning to understand you must go back to better days...days when you sat around the fire. (Take another break. Go see Julie Andrews who will lead the group in 'In the evening by the Moonlight', the Stephen Foster rouser.)

End of Part One of Test No. 9

End of Chapter 18

"DEZCARTES"

Dezcartes is a bit of a philosopher. He was given experimental injections on Plum Island and ended up with the powers of human reasoning. Here, he is contemplating being a rat and has concluded, "I am a rat, therefore, I am a rat." Some say Dezcartes reasoning powers have exceeded those of Homo Sapiens.

CHAPTER 19

HEADACHE

"We need new rules for war. The old ones don't work."
-Excerpted from https://notesfromtheroomofwonder.com

Mathuzala came down from the cloud one day, lit up a Lucky, and told me, in a pontificating manner, that in his roamings he had learned all major social and political movements go through three basic phases. The first phase being: Ridicule. "Very powerful, this phase." (Puff) Then comes: Discussion. (Phase Two) You know, where people actually talk about the issues involved. And finally: Implementation. (Phase Three)

(Excuse me if this seems like heady stuff; but Mathuzala does not rummage about in the cloud observing 'Housewives of Atlanta', or 'House Rats of Bayonne')

So: Back to the subject of Movements and their implementation. If those in opposition to a movement are still in the Ridicule phase, while those in favor are well past Discussion and have embarked on Implementation - well, then the Ridiculers are on the losing end of the stick. And they will get run over while they are chortling and looking the other way.

For example, you can see this playing out - right now - with the Ridiculers regarding how we humans take care of our physical selves. There should have been a robust health movement afoot for many years, but for the Ridiculers. "Eat smaller portions," Nutritionists have been saying. "Drink less than a bucket sized container of sugared soda. ...Eat organic. …Stay away from chemicalized meats…. Exercise more." These ideas have been scoffed and sniggered at for decades. And while the Ridiculers, for whatever reasons, scorned the suggestions for healthful social changes, we grew fat, fatter and unhealthy. Corporations, who have lawyers, who are people too - say they are safeguarding our right to do whatever we want to do to ourselves - as long as we pay for it. Compound this with an ample supply of Civil Libertarians who protect our right to choose whatever we want to, to gorge ourselves at will with giant sized portions of whatever we desire to stuff into our mouths. Well, these Ridiculers, in disguise of good business and defenders of our god given free will to damage ourselves, are legion and often have the *'Mo'*.

But, some of us then slowly enter into Phase Two, and *talk* about proper diet, talk about it and discuss it, until the cows come home. 'Eating Right' talk on the talk shows, radio, infomercials, books - on and on. …and then a few brave souls begin to move on to Phase Three: Implementation. And suddenly there is a germ of a movement. And, hopefully the proper diet Ridiculers will be rendered clogged from eating plastic and chemicalized meats. And the *Mo* will be no mo.

(My bad, not a good time to make with the puns.)

There are not only Good Health Ridiculers out there – causing throwback problems, there are Climate Change Deniers, as well. They are the big deal dangerous Ridiculers of our time. Perhaps, we are about to emerge from the jeering and sniggering phase in this arena. But the big money today is still betting the Ridicule card.

You may think it preposterous when I say the rats are starting a sociopolitical movement. But I tell you they have passed through their own internal deriding moment. They have finely honed their theme during the discussion period - and are confident they are to be the next dominant species, which will lead us into the New Era.

And there are no more corrupt Errs. No more charismatic Baccis. The rats are as one. Make that: The rodents are as one.

As for the Chumpers:

Red has culled out those of us who were in it only for the money and who were secretly ridiculing the idea of the rats taking over. Speaking for myself on this matter, I have made so much money from the constant rat deposits that I now can afford to rise above the base material acquisitive activities which drive so many. I'll admit it is easy when it is easy, but there you have it - which is to say: I am almost totally with the program.

Anyway, the Discussion Phase is near over. The *movement* is in the cusp, moiling between chatter and implementation. (a.k.a. Phases Two and Three)

You should see some headlines I have cut out from major U.S. newspapers - just to help bring you up to speed, to make you "Au Courant", as Eloise would say.

The below is from 'The Paper of Record'. (You know the one.) The headline was so big it covered the entire top of the fold.

CITY'S POWER GOES DOWN MILLIONS SUFFER!

WEAK INFRASTRUCTURE BLAMED!!!

You must have read about the power outage. New Yorkers, you know, are wallowing in the period before Ridicule. This is best known as the time of the Disbelieving Uninformed. Manhattanites tend to believe the power company has not poured enough money into its plant and equipment to serve the community. Maybe the company is guilty of this, maybe not - but it is the rats who have nibbled the power to 'off' - and that is a fact.

No one wants to know.

By the way, the rats are content that no one is pointing fingers at them. They harbor no desire for recognition of their accomplishments. They take no pride in little victories. Win. Win. In the new rules of war, one of the prime axioms is: Start it; but don't declare it. Don't let the opposition know who the opponent is - for as long as you can get away with it. Pretty smart, huh? No blustering ego. No flag waving. No flags at all, come to think of it.

Here is another headline. This from the NYC paper owned by the real estate guy from Boston. It covered the whole front page - with a few sports scores at the bottom for the athletic and or gaming minded reader.

FLASH CRASH DRIVES MARKET DOWN BIG TIME!!!

POSSIBLE CYBERTERRORIST ATTACK ON FREE MARKETS!!!

YANKS IN SERIES!!! .... GIANTS BLOW IT IN O.T. 20-23
.....Did not even break spread!!!!

The corresponding article attached to the above headline regarding the stock market goes like this:

"Yesterday afternoon, at ten minutes after two, the New York Stock Exchange suffered a flash crash caused by a shutdown of computer services to the Floor. At twenty minutes after two, the Market, having dropped over two thousand points, was shut down. The N. Y. Stock Exchange Chairman says the Exchange will re-open for business today as soon as buyers can be matched to sellers. It is estimated an excess of twenty billion dollars' worth of wealth has been sweated out of the market in the last hour and a half of trading and non-trading.

"As for the question of 'Who is responsible for this?' Experts tell us it is most likely caused by hackers from the Ukraine. Or, perhaps, a Muslim terrorist group, maybe a twelve- year old kid in a garage...."

Well, if you believe these Cock-a- Mamie ideas, I have a bridge in Brooklyn to sell you.

The above piece must have been written by an intern. That is a problem with the press nowadays, everything is written by interns and the writers don't know anything about anything. It is not merely the internet that is putting the newspapers out of business. But I digress.

There are more. Look at this one (Upstate NY paper):

NUCLEAR FUEL RODS OVERHEAT!!

FACILITY SHUT DOWN!!!

CATSKILLS ON ALERT!!!

(And then this at the bottom of the front page):
Antique Road Auction coming to Town!!! Bring your family curios to the school gym by Thursday

- -

The accompanying article prattled on about how the melt- down could possibly hurt tourism and how many jobs could be lost, or downgraded, and maybe people would have to drink out of plastic bottles for a while - that is, if the situation were not handled immediately. "This could be quite a headache," opined the mayor of Hudson.

Something to note: These three events occurred one day after another - exactly at ten minutes past two, each day. Did anyone notice that? No, I don't think so.

How about you? Do you think: 'Weak infrastructure?' Possibly. 'Ukrainian hackers?' Possibly. 'A nuclear headache?' Could be. 'Rats in the wires?' "Don't be ridiculous", you say.

...And that is the problem. Well, part of the problem. Another chunk of the problem is: The rats are much enthused over their cause. And they know their cause to be righteous. Talk about headaches. Nothing more bothersome than a self-righteous adversary that you do not even know about.

End of Chapter 19

"THE NELSONS"

Meet the Nelsons. Mr. Nelson job is to nibble on electrical cords over at the nuclear facility in upper New York State. His whole family can join him at the feast – anytime they want to – for free!

CHAPTER 20

CHOCOLATE

"I have been to the cloud - and I have seen what
there is to see. It is a lot to absorb."
-Excerpted from https://notesfromtheroomofwonder.com

So.

It has begun. The period of The Nibblings.

And no one knows about it. People are too busy with their own lives to see what is happening around them. The inconveniences of black-outs, nuclear rods over-heating, flash-crashes, movie streaming outages, airplanes falling out of the skies, malfunctions ad nauseam, are generally tolerated as a form of macabre news entertainment; someone else's problems, narrow misses to their own comforts - and are thought to be due to poor government, or bad luck, or mother nature, terrorists, foreign nationals, corruption...those kind of things. The humans point fingers in many directions - but not to the correct one, the one down under their feet. Nobody is going there.

The rats have fired the first salvo and have locked their munchings on 'fully automatic'. The constant nibbling is cutting a wide swath. They are biting by small nibs. Chewing off more than we can handle. Tiny morsels of creative destruction, adding up to huge mounds of serious consequences.

Philosophical types may consider the present time in which we live to be a discombobulating of known and untold past events which explain where we are and where we are going. ... But *wrong-o*. *New* forces are at work and will alter everything. This was made clear to me by Mathuzala only the other night.

I entered his room carrying the latest headlines, which were screaming of collapses, cave-ins and what have you (a.k.a. little Rat Victories). I saw my beloved leader resting quietly behind a heavily scented blue haze.

"Do not be alarmed, my Little Pea-pod. I am smoking marijuana for medical purposes only." It seemed to be working, for Mathuzala spoke without pain and was almost giddy. The small coterie of Ma-STERs surrounding him appeared to be benefitting from the residual medicinal value of the blue haze as well.

It was at this meeting where I was truly inducted into the fellowship of the Rats, where I became forever the *One*: the tried and true Chumper of Chumpers; no longer in it for the wealth or the glory. No longer any little smidgeons of doubts – nothing held back. For it was that night when Mathuzala took me into his deepest confidence and showed me The Perspective of The Others.

He took a deep drag from his petite-sized joint and held the medicated breath in his lungs for the longest of time. His little peepers slowly opened wide and in a soothing whisper he commanded: "Look into my eyes. Chzleek. Cough, cough."

Yes. Mathuzala hypnotized me. And in so doing he took me into his mind, into the mind-set of the rodent world. I saw what he saw, what *they* saw.

Here is some of what I experienced that night. The night of Nevermore, The night of all things both great and small. The night I saw the punishments of the Scrolls, the night I realized we were not the captains of our fates, nor the masters of our souls:

Mathuzala took me up into the ever-expanding Cloud, the mega giga, supra cumulus nimbulus of the infinite Cloud. It is as you would imagine in appearance. It is very white and fluffy. Mostly pure white intangible fluffs of cloudy stuff, soft and refreshingly cool fluffs which are constantly, and in slow-motion, moving, and diving gently into themselves; like a batter of some kind of heavenly cookie dough. There are some areas, however, which are beginning to gain a tactile substance, a tacky feel to the hardening fluff - sort of like a soft steel wool. These fluffs are less white - and remind me of the dirty snow you might see by a heavily trafficked roadside. These regions are growing, but to date they are not a significant portion of the Cloud.

Frequently, if you were to look quickly, you would see all the colors of the rainbow - and more, colors you have never seen before - up there, occasionally sparkling and whisking off the whiter tufts which turn and dip back down into the deep recesses of the cumuli. It is dreamy really.

It is cool up there, with a real feel of about fifty-six degrees. As for the smell, the after-shave Old Spice comes to mind.

How big is the Cloud? It is way bigger than the Gyre out in the Pacific - that glob of a plastic island forming out of tossed away garbage – which, it is said, would take all the navies in the world, with all their nets, thirty years to transport its pieces to the nearest shore for re-cycling. It is bigger than...well you get the point. And if you were to search for something in specific in the Cloud, ...well, it would be like trying to find a particular piece of hay in a field of genetically modified haystacks. And furthermore: The place is full of errors. More errors than the non-errors, as a matter of non-erroneous fact. My mentor told me it is easier to swallow the wondrous false, than the wondrous truth, so you have to really be careful what you take in. These errors are becoming toxic and are beginning to debauch the Garden —at the risk of waxing poetic. Nevertheless, Mathuzala knew his way around up there and he started off by taking me way back.

Back before Mahalleel, before the time of Seth and his parents.

Back before that line of the fourth mid-creation, there were rodents and they were abounding. And there were Men then, too. Those were simpler times. Hard times for Man. But he endured.

Way back then, for the rats, it was a good epoch. Often, as if remora, they lived off the benefits of mankind. Much like Spanish moss lives off the tropical tree, as the pilot fish lives off the great whale - the rodent, in many ways, thrived off the tailings in the footpath of mankind.

In those early days Men were healthier than those who currently inhabit the earth. Nonetheless, it was a difficult life. Running around all day looking for something to eat, always on the lookout for everything that wanted to eat them. No fire, no easy access to water, no clothes - no nothing, really. Just learning how to stand upright was quite a feat.

And then in a flash of intuitive insight, in a magical moment, Man, with his puny brain, invented the Stone. Yes. Man discovered he could use the Stone to bop something over the head with - and maybe eat that something. ...and then he learned he could throw the stone...and hurt something with that toss. This was long before the discovery of fire. It was the Mother of all Inventions because everything invented after that was nothing more than a tweak of the original Stone; a labor-saving device.

For the many ensuing thousands of years, Man has been figuring out new ways to ease his labors - with resourceful variations of the Stone. A tool, a robot, hardware, software and malware; each, nothing but a Stone by another means.

At first, the Stone was good news for the rodents. Man multiplied, because of it - and grew food, thanks to it. And the rats, too, grew in number and benefitted from the abundance. The rats cleaned up, as it were.

In time Man formed caravans and went to faraway lands and established markets thither and yon. And the rats followed. And they prospered. All was good. And man sailed to new continents. And the rats sailed with them.

Oh, yes, there was the old misunderstanding with the plague business - but that is a blip in the past. The point to remember with the Plague hoo-ha is: Acting on false assumptions can lead to terrible consequences.

Many humans died because man blamed rats: False assumption. They could have saved millions of lives if they had gone after those diseased fleas instead. Insects are another problem. From up in the Cloud you can see their growing menace. Back to that issue another time. (Much is gleaned about the insect threat in the cloud and much is revealed on this subject in https://notesfromtheroomofwonder.com)

Anyway, Man has this recurring tendency to act out on false assumptions, because there is no one around to set him straight and no authority to adjust his thinking. At least there was no one, not until now.

So...

Man had escorted the rats to the four corners of the earth - always providing easy sustenance for them. It was good for a while. A good deal for both parties. Then it went wrong.

The part of the Cloud I was in at this time turned from a nimbulus shape to a cumulus-nimbus configuration. The ambiance changed dramatically. It was no longer the fluffy white stuff I rhapsodized about a few pages back. If you were to imagine what it looked like in animal form (You know, the way children try to see animals in the clouds. Try to remember when you were a kid...) You might envision a million snake-head fish all moiling about up there, eating each other and breeding insatiably with the rest. There was a shower of lightning bolts spurting arc flashes and there were horrid, ear drum bursting thunderclaps. And then I saw black lightening. Flashes of darkness which almost blinded the eyes. Black bolts arcing from one to another. I counted the seconds from the black flash to the thunder; the bolts were only a couple of miles away from us. Quite scary, actually.

Enough of my fears. To continue with what I came to see from up there with Mathuzala:

... Over the millennia, Man brought his bags of stones with him wherever he went. And in so doing, he fouled his own nest, which is also the nest of The Others. The humans fought amongst themselves over territories, commodities and dominance. Dominance became the imperative. Dominance meant Control. Man had become a Control Freak. And he used his Stones accordingly, but the Stones have gone freaking out of control and man is about to freak out. I'm not kidding; you can see this from up there. You can see all the agitation, all the wrestling around down on the ground.

The gift of the Stone has been desecrated. Its purpose was to ease man's burden. If 'Success' is life without work - and it is, then: Work is failure.

(You never see rats work, oh no. Rats live by the Lilies of the Field ethic, the way the birds and butterflies do. They neither toil, nor labor, nor fear. Well, they do fear now, but not because of not working.)

As I was saying, I learned in the cloud that work is failure.

...After many millennia and after millions of tweaks on the Stone: Man had failed. Failed to achieve life without toil. And now he has failed to provide for himself and is using up the earth in his madness. Billions starve and go thirsty. What good are the Stones now?

Worse, than no good, they are toxic. It is safer in the Cloud than it is down here even though the Cloud itself is beginning to act up. But the Cloud is virtually not real, and you can't hide out up there forever.

Oddly, the time has come where there are not enough jobs for man, and yet there is much work to be done - on the one hand. And on the other hand, no one wants to pay for the work to be done. And on the third hand, no one wants to do the work no one wants to pay for anyway. It is puzzlement to those who have not thought it through enough. Once in the cloud, you can see 'the jobs' are never coming back; and without a job, you can become poor, and if you are poor you can't buy anything, and if ninety-nine percent of you can't buy anything, then the economy goes down the rat-hole, pardon my French, and the bad news is: (And you could see this, too, if you were high in the Cloud) The struggles will not be over jobs, gasoline or food for the hungry. No. The struggles will be the thrashings for the survival of the wealthiest, which are out of control with their latest, *au courant* version of Stones in *their* piles which are carrying death and extinction to The Others.

That night, Mathuzala and I sifted through the day's trillions of bits of information, the gazillions of e-mails sent to and fro, read the millions of headlines, watched global news shows hosted in the many post-Babylonian languages, listened to the countless prayers of man... And the digest of all this is: Man is losing his grip and is getting ready for a spoil - big time.

"Someone has to pay...and it might as well be somebody else." Men the world over are saying.

The fighting will begin in earnest - unless something can be done. And what can be done, can be done by first nibbling away at the Stones.

This is what I saw through Mathuzala's eyes that night. I now knew what the rats knew and felt. And I was one with them.

When I came down from the Cloud I had an uncontrollable urge for vanilla ice cream with hot fudge sauce, topped with peanuts. Incredibly, Eloise, knowing my every need, was right there with exactly that: A Hot Fudge Tin Roof Sundae - and two spoons.

End of Chapter 20

"HANK"

Hank has a nose for what's going on. He smells the winds are blowing in his favor – it's the stench of the City, and that means the Humans are losing control and his kind are taking over. If you were a Rat, you'd be happy too.

CHAPTER 21, PART A

CANDLE

"The more you changed, the less has remained the same. You have changed everything, and nothing remains the same. The old truths have changed. You have even changed your Scripture. You turned the decent suggestion of 'Go forth and do the math' into the stupid and perilous idea of: 'Go forth and multiply'....and indeed, you have multiplied. The intended advice had been warped in the translation....and the consequences of this error are greater than you would think. If you had done the math, you would have known you could not afford to have 4 billion people on Earth – let alone 7 billion plus – and mounting.

"...And now you can't even do the basic math without your little phones.

You people do not even know how to start a fire, if needed, or sit in the dark - in silence. Forget about silence. Most of you do not know how to grow food.

"...We have arrived to the point where we see your gene pool has been diminished and perverted, causing you to want things you don't need and need things you don't want – all this re-confirms neither you, nor we - can afford your civilization, any more..."

-Excerpted from https://notesfromtheroomofwonder.com

"P.S.-Your cerebral cortex resembles the marine ragtime worm or vice-versa - for what that is worth."

(ibid)

Ring hard the bell. Rewrite the book. Light again the candle. We have begun a new era. It is not too late to save the day, to correct our way...to put things on the right path. Mathuzala and his Ma-STERs came up with a Two-Pronged Plan which would - make that: *which is* succeeding. You are already acquainted with Prong One: The Nibblings. You might be aware how this front is progressing, if you would read the news.

Now we have Prong Two: The Hearts & Minds. My, oh yes. It was while roaming around in the cloud when Mathuzala came to the realization that the best way to win - and *to keep the win* in the battle for domination - was to captivate the Hearts & Minds of the humans. (Addressing your minds is where the Marine Ragtime worm reference bears some significance).

To my great honor: I was appointed the Chief Intervener, (a.k.a. Executive Producer) for this Great Humanitarian and Interspecies Melding.

We turned Eloise's apartment into the vital communications hub from which all enterprises were generated. These were exciting times.

What the Ma-STERs had realized was the Rats had suffered a bad rap with humans. This perplexed the Ma-STERs at first, because with all the disgusting things humans do - which are too many to mention here, the humans were not disgusted with themselves. However, a little skittering over food leavings in the dark, or some night scratchings in the walls - humans would go berserk; immediately searching for brooms, clubs and chemicals. The end result was: The rats decided it was necessary to change the human's perception of the entire rodent world. The trick, of course, would be to do this without changing rodent behavior; for not one rat, nor its cousin, has ever been proven guilty of ever doing anything wrong, criminal or otherwise. We are not talking propaganda here. Oh, no.

We are talking more than that.

Our first project was a pilot of a children's television show. We created a digitized version of our dear Petal. She virtually teaches your children how to count and do their little alphabetty letters. A digitalized Petal brings Julie Andrews out upon occasion and Julie teaches the children, your children, how to dance - and when to dance. The network Executives love the pilot of 'The Itty-Bitty Ratty Baby Sitty' and are in a bidding war right now over who gets to show it. Of course, some of the executives are Chumpers, so this project will go smoothly.

Concurrently, we are working on a show which will compete in the time slot with the big FOX and MSNBC talk rant news evening shows. The format will have a small pack of Ma-STERs talking, cheeks and all - about all the horrible things man is doing to himself and the planet. They will do this in a laugh riot, humorous way because humans take in their news better if it is in a jokey métier than if it were represented in raw, unvarnished, factual truth. Test audiences love this contrivance. They assume the rats are some sort of a clever Muppet ventriloquist assemblage - which makes the whole shtick easily digestible for the young minded adults, who are so predominant in today's vibrant consumer market. Everybody who is anybody will want to be a guest of 'The Ma-STERs' RAT-A-TAT NEWS HOUR': Rock Stars, Movie Actors, and Celebs of all walks - even people who are not yet Chumpers. We expect monster ratings. The telecast will be available in your home viewing package sometime late summer.

It does not stop at TV. We are coming out with a major motion picture release in the next fall. You know what a pitch is? A pitch is a thirty second presentation which tells the Money what the movie is about. The pitch has to be good to get the Money. Here was our pitch:

"...The world is being threatened by insects. Insects are eating everything and growing in horrifying numbers - the combined weight of ants alone exceeds that of all the humans, no matter how fat some humans are. There are over 10 million to the 24th power of ants - and growing - on the planet. Scary, huh? Well! This young married couple (Good for PG-13) is being eaten out of house and home and there are bedbugs in the mattresses and the bedbugs, too, are beginning to grow to the 24th power and we see the insects are about to take over the world and (luckily) the lovey-dovey young couple joins up with a pack of rats who are fighting insects themselves so they can keep their own place bug free...and the rats and the couple kill bugs for over two hours and there are car chases and a building explodes with a lot of shattering glass and the President of the United states orders the CIA to stop hounding the couple and gives them a medal of honor instead and the rats get medals too - because they are heroes - as they stopped the onslaught of insects throughout the Northeast and the President sets the couple up as head of a three letter agency to fight the fight throughout the country. (We are talking Sequels. Maybe this would be a made for TV, many Seasoned, multi-Episoded kind of thing))

"Thirty seconds."

So, what if you don't like the pitch. We already have the Money.

I wanted Eloise and me to play the couple, but the truth is we are too old for the part. The truth hurts, sometimes; but I can take it. I am hoping to get the role of the President of the United States. Julie Andrews will do the music. She is planning some show stopping original numbers. We'll dance 'em out of the aisles.

Distribution is in hand. The heads of two major theater groups are well entrenched Chumpers. The show will be released next summer; subsequent to 4-wall promos, internet advertising and talk show hype. Netflix, Amazon, Alibaba, Apple, Hawah (or whatever that Chinese telecom company is called) and all the outer-channels are signing on. People are already mentioning Oscars - even though the screenplay is still a work in progress.

GAMES. Talk about fun. We have contacted game designers in Japan and M.I.T. They have created some of the most challenging, thrilling and inter-active games ever produced. Also, we will have Humans playing virtual chess against Rats – and sometimes winning. Humans playing virtual Poker against Rats – and winning real money from time to time. All kinds of fun games for every generation. Rights are being auctioned as we write, and the first installment will be on the racks in time for Black Thursday. And they will be sold Cheap. Loss leaders. What do we care?

Caution: Under 17 will not be permitted to play the more violent games. In some of our exciting products - in order to proceed to a higher level - one must kill bad humans. A digitized Red will assist you if you convince her you have the integrity to carry on. If you fail at certain levels, however, Red will do you in, in a horrible way. (Virtually speaking, of course) The blood and flesh splatter on the demos are quite astonishing. In order to get to the highest rung, up in the cloud, where Mathuzala, the Wise One resides, one must surmount incredible obstacles, which are: Corruption, Pollution, Aggression and Toxic Waste - all personified by zombie-like looking humans. 'RATS, The Deliverance, #1' is a 'Must Have' and everybody will be playing it, or they will be out of it. You watch.

We will have: Phone apps, web-casts, pod-casts, blogs, daily u-tubes, Twitters, Tweets, e-mails, Tic-Tocs, streamings - and more. All of this to influence the Human's (positive) attitude towards their newest best friends – the Rats.

We will even have an old-fashioned radio show where we talk about a friendly mid-west community with a folksy and generally agreeable collection of humans and animals, mostly rodents. Every Sunday night there will be a segment where an old rat and a young girl in a posh hotel solve a crime, in a humorous way - all accompanied by clever sound effects; like scratching fingernails on blackboards to simulate the sound of cute baby rats at play in the basement. We don't expect much of a following here - but we think the older Boomers, who are dying out, will stay tuned. Older Boomers like to harken back to the never existed simpler times.

As for the written word: We know printed news is on the way out - and we will not fight the current trend. Nonetheless, a *book* of high literary value is being put together. I have taken the musings of Mathuzala and am assembling them in a two-volume oeuvre titled: *Principia Rodentia* - for those few who are of an intellectual and academic bent. It may be my life's intellectual achievement.

There is more, much more - for winning the Hearts & Minds of a heartless, small-minded species is a long and difficult slog.

These are early days. If you have any ideas which may be of use to our cause, please contact us through https://notesfromtheroomofwonder.com. If you would like to be considered for membership into the elite corps of Chumpers, feel free to contact us through that same site. Just click: 'Register', then sign in and then go to: 'Membership' - off to the right side of your screen.

End of Chapter 21, part A.

"GINGER & FRED"

Ginger and Fred are back from their cruise. All the Humans on board got sick from something in the food – the boat barely left the dock. No matter. Ginger & Fred, who have stronger stomachs than the humans, ate lot and had a good time. Tonight, it's off to the Rainbow Room.

CHAPTER 21 B

WHISPER

"One of your great Indian Chiefs once prophesied, 'What happens to the Beast will also happen to the Man'; but *I* know *what* happens to the Man will also happen to the Beast - so we must prevent the *'Big What'* from happening to the Man; in spite of himself."

-Excerpted from https:///notesfromtheroomofwonder.com

(The following is from the transcripts of a recent Chumpers' 'Town Hall' - held in the Grand Ballroom at the Plaza [You will note we have moved up from the sub-sub-basement. FYI, the event began at 3:00 in the morning. We like to get off to an early start, before the roiling humans try to shake off their torpors.] I was the Master of Ceremonies and answered some of the questions myself. Mathuzala was Skyped, Zoomed and WhatsApped in and he fielded a few grounders from his hospice. A side table topped with a small pack of Ma-STERs responded to the crowd, as well. Red passed the microphone from Chumper to Chumper. Eloise was the hostess. She provided Tea and Prune-crumb-cakes to the Ma-STERs' panel. These meetings were well received by one and all.)

Me:

... "We will take your questions now. (To give you a visual, I was wearing a form-fitting, long sleeved, black, t-shirt. I frequently strolled the stage as I spoke. I learned this technique from watching self-help gurus on TV) ...

"Please stand and speak clearly into the mike. State your name and affiliation. We have an open-door policy here, so feel free to speak up. Don't be afraid to bring up any doubts or uncertainties which may linger in your mind. You are among equals here. But remember: 'There is no such thing as a stupid question' - is one of the stupidest statements ever made. ... Just joking. ... You sir? Yes, you. ..."

(We have redacted [XXXX] the names of participants for security purposes.)

XXXX (State Congressman and gun control lobbyist):

"After the take-over will we be allowed to buy guns? What about semi-automatic rifles? Bump-Stocks? Silencers? Will we have to register? Or what...?"

Me:

"Good question. First let me emphasize, this is not a 'take-over', *per se*. This is a New Partnership. A partnership where humans and Rodents and other mammals will live in harmony. Remember that above all." (I could see Mathuzala on the jumbo-screen, nodding in approval of my statesman-like answer here.)

"As for guns and their accoutrements: The happy answer is: Yes! We can buy all the guns and gimmicks we want. There can be no lead in the bullets and the casings will have to be bio-degrade-able. As far as the subject of who gets to buy which guns, the rats will not enter this discussion. You should look into making those guns at home with the clever 3-d printers now available. If you want, we can arrange to deposit enough valuables at your doorsteps so you can buy one of these printers right after this meeting.

"It is for man to determine who gets the guns. The rats will not be involved in determining who is sane, mentally ill, or psychically impaired - for they often see humans make distinctions where there are none to be made. The rats do not understand how man, who has gone to the moon and developed language translator apps - how that same technologically intelligent creature can still argue over whether guns kill people, or people with guns kill people. But the rats will go along with these seemingly irresolvable issues - as long as men only kill each other with those contraptions. The days of killing other animals are coming to an end. And if man cannot live with that bargain - then all the guns will be removed - taken from their live, warm hands, as it were.

"...Yes?"

XXXX (Vice-president, Large NYC Bank):

"Is this 'Partnership' world-wide? I mean, are the rats 'all in', in this? I mean, if the degrading only happens here...well, we will lose market advantage...and how will we Americans stay Number One? Do you get my question...?"

… (Mathuzala breaks in)

Mathuzala:

"I'll take this one my Little Pea-pod....

"In response to 'Are we world-wide?' Yes. The rodents of the world are waiting for instructions, waiting for their orders. They are chomping at the bit, to use a turn of phrase. Chleezck. (Drag, Puff, Blow, Cough)

"It is true; recently we turned back our initial offensive wave. We did this to perfect and coordinate our plans. We have been practicing maneuvers right here in Manhattan. Our plan is Global. We have already nibbled a bit in Japan ... on one of their nuclear facilities ... and, testing the waters, we toppled a dam in California ...then, there was that episode in Iran that the humans think was a cyber-attack.

"But my travels in the Cloud have told me if we can 'make it' - or break it - in New York ...we can break it anywhere...and so, our efforts - for now, will be concentrated right here. When we fan out - you will be the first to know. Those of you who trade in the markets will be able to take advantage of this information for your own good. My recommendation would be to take aggressive short positions in the indexes at the appropriate time. We have even devised some derivatives so you can bet against the major hedge funds. You will clean up. (Drag, Puff, Chzleek)

"As for your question regarding how you stay 'Number One' - as you put it...you won't. There will be no more 'Number One' in the New Partnership. No need, for there will no longer be any super-power military nation states. You Chumpers, nevertheless, individually, will be able to glean as much wealth as you want, so that should be of some comfort to you.

Benedict, here, and his companion Eloise, are continuing to set up Chumper chapters throughout America and registration is quite robust as we speak. I am confident when we are ready to go national and world-wide...well, let us plainly say: It will be over - almost before you know it.

"Back to you Pea-pod." (Cough, hack, puff, blow)

Me:

"Thank you, Mathuzala. ...Let's see..." (Red moves to the center of the ball-room and hands the mike to a smartly dressed fashionista.) ..."You Ma'am. Yes, You"

XXXX (Proprietor, SOHO Fashion Boutique, Small Business Owner) ... "This is to the rats on the table. I mean, can I call you rats? I, I'm new at this and I don't mean to offend...but my question is...does this mean there are going to be rats all over the place? Are they ... Are you going to be mostly above ground now, or what? How do you communicate to each other? How do you make contact with your friends or whatever they are, if they are in California, let alone Japan? How do you travel long distances? I don't understand how any of this works..."

"CHEEEECK!" (A Loud feedback sounding noise filled the chamber. This came from one of the Ma-STERs on the table. He spoke into a tiny weensy little microphone so small you could hardly see. He looked wise, like a healthy Mathuzala. He had an imposing authority to him. He remained nameless)

"Why are these questions important? These questions of 'How'? For *what* is your need to understand these things? You individuals, you who do not know how cell-phones work. Yet you use them. You, who do not understand Electricity, the workings of the atoms, the very law of gravity. Yet you use these things. You, who have forgotten how to create a fire in the woods. ...and you, who are afraid to sit in the dark and in the stillness.

After all these years of studying us for your own purposes - now you want to know *how* we communicate, *how we travel*? Why? For what purpose?

"Know this: We do communicate with all of each other and we travel throughout.

"And yes, gradually we will be more above ground than we are at present; but when this is, you will be prepared for it and it will not be unacceptable to you. After all, we are winning 'The Hearts & Minds' - are we not? Cheeck." (And if you were there, you would have heard what sounded like rat laughter coming from the rat table.)

"Next question, please."

XXXX (Poetess and Free Thinker):

"This is to you Mr. Benedict, or 'My Little Pea-pod', or however you are called. My question to you is: How do you deal with your conscience? Betraying our species? I mean that is what we are doing isn't it? Like selling guns to the Indians...that sort of thing, only worse...I am having trouble living with the ethic here...the morality issue... and I want to know: How you cope...? (Red takes the mike away and I see her give a deep sniff behind the woman's shoulder and, in a quick moment of time, I see a flash of bicuspid)

Me:

"Fair question." "Fair. For me it was wealth and power in the beginning. But now I am convinced our cause is righteous. If we do not stop man from his present course – we will perish. So, we are doing good and great work - and putting a lot aside in the meantime. I'm coping very well, thank you. Eloise and I sleep very well at night. Next?"

XXXX (Television Advertising Executive, Time and Space sales):

"How is it that Rats can be all over television and in the movies and everywhere in the media and not be a known threat to human beings?"

Me:

"Another good question - and thank you for asking it. I have learned from Mathuzala's teachings - and I recommend you study his detailed thoughts as recorded on https://notesfromtheroomofwonder.com

(Ad Free) which speak to this very subject. What *I have* learned is we humans have this huge ego, almost narcissistic you might say, which prevents us from allowing ourselves to think any significant threat can come from anything but another human. ...We being so supreme and all. For example, if a computer system goes down - it has to be a human hacker. If a nuclear rod overheats, it is either because of labor incompetence or terrorism from some cult, nation state, or group of religious nuts. Same with airplanes falling out of skies, shut- downs on power grids and stock exchanges. We always blame each other. Big mistake. By the time the humans wake up to what they are really up against: Packs of rats - it will be too late. You, we, are hoisted by our own ego infested DNA.

"Next? Yes?"

The meeting went on for hours. It was both a struggle and great fun. A good demonstration of partnership in Democracy at work.

The early nibblings from our first troops on the ground had produced nice results. As for the Hearts & Minds; the opposition would soon begin to love us.

That night, Julie Andrews took us out with a rousing rendition of the Electric Cha-Cha Slide, intermixed with a smattering of Tupac Shakur. The room went wild – everybody who was anybody was on the floor.

Remember Curly? He was one-third of the trio which put me through the ringer with the poly. And then he shows up at one of our boot camps. Remember? Red had vetted him. He came up smelling like a rose. Even though Red is good, make that: *great* at what she does - I still did not trust the guy. Anyway, at the end of the meeting Curly came up to me and whispered in my ear, "Come with me."

I did no such thing. It was a mistake.

End of Chapter 21, part B

"MATHUZALA"

This is Mathuzala, before he became even more adorable. Before he grew a thick neck and put on five more pounds – all due to experiments perpetrated on him at the infamous Plum iIland. (For an updated photo of Mathuzala, go to; https://notesfromtheroomofwonder.com

CHAPTER 22

CUT

"Sometimes you walk into a store and you can tell the place is going to go out of business, like that film rental outfit that used to be everywhere. Or, those mega-bookstores, or big box discount electrical anchors. Sometimes you see a game and you know a team is going to lose when it walks on the field. Or, you see a hostage situation playing out on TV and you know the perp is a dead man walking. When the Enola Gay took off, they knew what the end story was before her wheels were up. What I am saying is: Sometimes It is over, even before it begins. And this is one of those times."

-Excerpted from https://notesfromtheroomofwonder.com

I am in a cell, in solitary, practicing mental exercises to retain my sanity. To keep my mind busy, I will describe to you my chamber and how I came to this unhappy place. My room is twelve feet wide by fifteen feet long. Battleship grey painted cinder block walls. One small open-air window high up near the ceiling. One light bulb hanging down on a black wire from overhead. There is a hole for a toilet in one corner of the floor. I am seated on a three-legged stool, dressed in a straitjacket. The jacket's sleeves are extended in length – beyond my hands - and are tied by strings behind my back.

A few days ago - I think it was - Curly came up to me and asked me to follow him - but I did not. I have a hazy recollection of Moe and Larry sneaking up on me later that night...in front of the Plaza by Central Park South... and ...then I wake up here, wherever I am. The soldiers, or whatever they are, have been asking me questions, stupid questions. They seem to think I am a terrorist, or a traitor, or something. They have read a lot of the Blog: https://notesfromtheroomofwonder.com

(Ad Free) – And your comments are appreciated. .Membership required to participate; but all personal information will be kept confidential and away from the hands of you know who.) Their suspicion is I am the blogger behind the blogs. Which is so much noise.

I am tired of referring to *them* as 'They', so I will refer to them as 'the idiots', or the like, from here on. The idiots do not understand Mathuzala's postings.

"Confess" They demand. But they do not know what it is I am to confess about.: "You have leaked information. ...to who? ... You sent coded messages to ...jihadi? or to the Russians? or to domestic terrorists? Tell us. ... Make it easy on yourself." On and on.

These morons, who are incapable of finding the sum of two plus two without a calculator, do not know what the Blog's NOTES are about - but they do know they do not like them. So, I am asked, ad nauseam, "Who is trying to take over the country? ... What is this *degrading* of civilized life? ...Who is coming? ... What are 'They' up to? ... When? ...Where will the attack come from? ... Who else is in on it? ... Name names." I am sleep deprived; but I take it for the cause.

Having listened to Mathuzala well - and as advised by him, I have told the truth, knowing the truth will not be believed. And the truth is: The rats have already taken control.

Congress is loaded with Chumpers, who, with their fellow lobbyists have rendered our government unfunded and inoperable. Chumper CEO's have driven corporations profit mad and the Fortune 500 have us strung out on I-phones, Apps, I-pads, TVs, Facebooks, U-Tubes and infinite streamings. We addictively entertain ourselves 24/7, staring into screens big and small while the rats take over the whole shebang. 'O.M.G., O.M.G! WHAT ARE YOU DOING?' I want to shout out to the human race every so often – and wake the humans and have them shrug off their stupors - but no one would pay attention. Am I conflicted? Yes. Nothing is as straight forward as it would seem.

Power stations of all kinds are frizzing out...did you see that Super

Bowl a while back? When all the lights went out? Have you forgotten that already? How about that? How compliant have we become? Turn out the lights - no complaints, as long as you show us stuff we can buy while we wait for 'them' to turn the lights back on - but soon the lights are not going to come back on.

Also, the rats know how to let us go crazy on our own right. They learned from the best, from us, from our experiments upon them. Have you not noticed civilian madness is on the rise? Uneducated youth. People with no homes, living on the streets. Looners waddling about with guns. Mass shootings, revenge slayings, random killings, suicides (rats do not commit suicide, no matter what) Has not the insanity arched to greater peaks? Do you think this is the natural path for the world's richest, most admired country in the history of man? I think not. We are eating so much poisoned food and drinking so much chemicalized water we cannot reason, reasonably anymore. It is the bottom of the ninth and the rats are the only ones on the scoreboard.

Meanwhile, the interrogators ask me about the Russians, Muslims and PETA - yes, PETA.

I have told my inquisitors everything I have told you earlier in these pages. The stupes do not believe me. I told them our time will neither end with a bang, nor with a whimper – but in disbelief. The idiots say I am speaking gobbledy-gook. ...Their threat is they can keep me here forever, it being legal to do so 'in the name of National Security'.

Massaging my temples, I visualize the day I will return to Eloise and have ice cream with her and work with Red, and dance the Inter-species Cha-Cha Electric Slide with Julie Andrews, and work with my fellow Chumpers and bring mankind to a safer, gentler climb - and away from destroying itself.

But for now, I sit alone on my three-legged stool.

You remember, don't you? ... I told you earlier about all the studies Mathuzala and I have been horrified by? Studies which had been conducted on rats, hoping to find out how long it took to drive them insane. Experiments by grad students hiding the Rat's cheese, keeping rats in solitary confinement, continually, loudly playing rap music in the rats' tiny ears. Many, many such trials. And the rats learned how to endure all this. I have learned from them. Here is what *I* do: I think. I take myself out of here by thinking - and I keep my sanity.

For example, sometimes I take a mental cut to the fellow in the next cell, if there is a fellow in the next cell, if there is a next cell - and I wonder if he is more miserable than me. Perhaps, he has never been anywhere and now he is stuck in a cinder blocked cell and will never get to see such as the likes of The Plaza and Eloise and all the good things in life, which I have seen.

Or, am I the more wretched one because I have seen it all and I now sit here deprived of everything? ...and then I think that particular scenario I just imagined did not take up enough time to keep me from going crazy.

Now I'll conjure up a third cell:

In this room I see a shaft of light coming over me and making me warm and - suddenly, the light envelopes me and draws me up in the Cloud. I am roaming with Mathuzala, and ... and, I see Bacci over there, and in a flash of intuitive insight I understand she may never have been quite real. She is a sort of a digitalized figment of a hypnotizing hologram floating around. Did Mose & Err create her? ...Wait? Who was that then who killed Bacci? Was he for real? Was he ever really a Governor of California, as our memories say? Or was it just a bad dream? Even though Bacci may never have actually existed, she is still in the Cloud. For nothing, not even *no thing* - ever gets totally deleted.

Now we are looking down from the Cloud at mankind and we see all the havoc and pollution and danger man is generating. I see my interrogators who I note are looking into their I-phones, checking weather apps and tweeting to their friends.

Wait! Down there in the three-letter agency. ...Yes, it is Moe on his PC and he is looking at and sexting a young naked girl who is not does not happen to be his wife...and, oh my God! There is Larry watching a U-tube piece which is nothing but streamed, X-rated bathroom humor - on a constant loop. And these are the guys who grabbed me and had me detained and eventually tied to this three-legged stool?

The rooms of my mind cascade back to where I am sitting. ...only two minutes have elapsed since I first told you where I am. The mind travels faster than the speed of time, no?

I can take this, for there is a fourth room, *der vunderkammer*, where I can go. Let us now cut to the Room of Wonder Room of my mind. I have decorated it with images of everything I have ever seen which has caused me to smile or given me any modicum of pleasure. The air is clean. The lights are soft and low. The great books of man fill handsome bookshelves. There are maps of the world, the stars and galaxies. A solarium. An astrolabe. An Arabian elephant water clock in a gigantic, antique French vitrine. Paintings by the Old Masters adorn the walls. A stuffed alligator hangs down from the ceiling. Better yet, the entire ceiling is festooned with seashells from the seven oceans and fossils from the lost continent. Birds of Paradise perch freely on the rafters. Out the big bay window is a spectacular view of the sea and beyond the horizon I can see a majestic mountain range with snow-capped peaks. I see no man-made structures outside my window, no malls, and no big box stores. It is secure in here and I can come back whenever I want. I can lock my interrogators out.

But I cannot stay in the 'Room of Wonder' forever. I must return to do my work. Think. Think. How can I get out of my prison?

Suddenly, I am aware of a faint tugging on the back side of my jacket. I hear the welcome scratching. I feel nibbling on the strings knotted behind my back.

Then, on the floor, staring up at me is a little creature that looks like he could be an offspring of my old friend Mathuzala. He takes a puff from his little cigarette and says,

"Hi, Uncle Pea-pod."

"Hi, back." I say.

End of Chapter 22.

…And End of: THE RAT PAPERS

"MATHUZALAS' GRANDCHILDREN"

See *(some of)* Mathuzalas' grandchildren. See them run things. Collectively, they know more than there is to know. If "Knowledge is Power"; they rule!

Printed in the United States
By Bookmasters